The Critics on J. G. BALLARD

"Ballard is one of the brightest new stars in post-war fiction. This tale of strange and terrible adventure in a world of steaming jungles has an oppressive power reminiscent of Conrad."

—KINGSLEY AMIS

"Science fiction suffers a sea-change into something rich and strange. Ballard's potent symbols of beauty and dismay inundate the reader's mind. It's most haunting: really the very best Ballard—which is very good indeed."

—BRIAN ALDISS

The above two quotations are from the English reviews of Ballard's latest novel, *The Drowned World*, which was a critical sensation upon its publication earlier this year in London.

PASSPORT
TO ETERNITY

J. G. Ballard

A BERKLEY MEDALLION BOOK
published by
BERKLEY PUBLISHING CORPORATION

CONTENTS

The Man on the 99th Floor	5
Thirteen to Centaurus	12
Track 12	32
The Watch-Towers	37
A Question of Re-Entry	62
Escapement	91
The Thousand Dreams of Stellavista	103
The Cage of Sand	121
Passport to Eternity	143

ACKNOWLEDGMENTS

"The Man on the 99th Floor" published in *New Worlds Science Fiction*
Copyright © 1962, by Nova Publications Ltd., London
"Thirteen to Centaurus" published in *Amazing Fact and Science Fiction*
Copyright © 1962, by Ziff-Davis Publishing Company
"Track 12" published in *New Worlds Science Fiction*
Copyright © 1958, by Nova Publications Ltd., London
"The Watch-Towers" published in *Science Fantasy*
Copyright © 1962, by Nova Publications Ltd., London
"A Question of Re-Entry" published in *Fantastic Stories*
Copyright © 1963, by Ziff-Davis Publishing Company
"Escapement" published in *New Worlds Science Fiction*
Copyright © 1956, by Nova Publications Ltd., London
"The Thousand Dreams of Stellavista" published in
Amazing Fact and Science Fiction
Copyright © 1962, by Ziff-Davis Publishing Company
"The Cage of Sand" published in *New Worlds Science Fiction*
Copyright © 1962, by Nova Publications Ltd., London
"Passport to Eternity" published in *Amazing Fact and Science Fiction*
Copyright © 1962, by Ziff-Davis Publishing Company

BERKLEY EDITION, SEPTEMBER, 1963

BERKLEY MEDALLION BOOKS are published by
Berkley Publishing Corporation,
15 East 26th Street, New York 10, New York

Printed in the United States of America

THE MAN ON THE 99TH FLOOR

ALL DAY Forbis had been trying to reach the 100th floor. Crouched at the foot of the short stairway behind the elevator shaft, he stared up impotently at the swinging metal door onto the roof, searching for some means of dragging himself up to it. There were eleven narrow steps, and then the empty roof deck, the high grilles of the suicide barrier and the open sky. Every three minutes an airliner went over, throwing a fleeting shadow down the steps, its jets momentarily drowning the panic which jammed his mind, and each time he made another attempt to reach the doorway.

Eleven steps. He had counted them a thousand times, in the hours since he first entered the building at ten o'clock that morning and rode the elevator up to the 95th floor. He had walked the next four—the floors were fakes, offices windowless and unserviced, tacked on merely to give the building the cachet of a full century—then waited quietly at the bottom of the final stairway, listening to the elevator cables wind and drone, hoping to calm himself. As usual, however, his pulse started to race, within two or three minutes was up to one hundred and twenty. When he stood up and reached for the hand-rail something clogged his nerve centres, caissons settled on to the bed of his brain, rooting him to the floor like a lead colossus.

Fingering the rubber cleats on the bottom step, Forbis glanced at his wrist-watch. 4.20 p.m. If he wasn't careful someone would climb the stairs up to the roof and find him there—already there were half a dozen buildings around the city where he was persona non grata, elevator boys warned to call the house detectives if they saw him. And there were not all that many buildings with a hundred floors. That was part of his obsession. There had to be one hundred exactly.

Why? Leaning back against the wall, Forbis managed to ask himself the question. What role was he playing out, searching the city for hundred-storey sky-scrapers, then performing this obsessive ritual which invariably ended in the

5

same way, the final peak always unscaled? Perhaps it was some sort of abstract duel between himself and the architects of these monstrous piles (dimly he remembered working in a menial job below the city streets—perhaps he was rebelling and re-asserting himself, the prototype of urban ant-man trying to over-topple the totem towers of Megalopolis?)

Aligning itself on the glideway, an airliner began its final approach over the city, its six huge jets blaring. As the noise hammered across him, Forbis pulled himself to his feet and lowered his head, passively letting the sounds drive down into his mind and loosen his blocked feedbacks. Lifting his right foot, he lowered it on to the first step, clasped the rail and pulled himself up two steps.

His left leg swung freely. Relief surged through him. At last he was going to reach the door! He took another step, raised his foot to the fourth, only seven from the top, then realised that his left hand was locked to the hand-rail below. He tugged at it angrily, but the fingers were clamped together like steel bands, the thumbnail biting painfully into his index tip.

He was still trying to unclasp the hand when the aircraft had gone.

Half an hour later, as the daylight began to fade, he sat down on the bottom step, with his free right hand pulled off one of his shoes and dropped it through the railing into the elevator shaft.

Vansittart put the hypodermic away in his valise, watching Forbis thoughtfully.

"You're lucky you didn't kill anyone," he said. "The elevator cabin was thirty storeys down, your shoe went through the roof like a bomb."

Forbis shrugged vaguely, letting himself relax on the couch. The Psychology Department was almost silent, the last of the lights going out in the corridor as the staff left the medical school on their way home. "I'm sorry, but there was no other way of attracting attention. I was fastened to the stair-rail like a dying limpet. How did you calm the manager down?"

Vansittart sat on the edge of his desk, turning away the lamp.

"It wasn't easy. Luckily Professor Bauer was still in his office and he cleared me over the phone. A week from now, though, he retires. Next time I may not be able to bluff my way through. I think we'll have to take a more direct line. The police won't be so patient with you."

"I know. I'm afraid of that. But if I can't go on trying my brain will fuse. Didn't you get any clues at all?"

Vansittart murmured noncommittally. In fact the events had followed exactly the same pattern as on the three previous occasions. Again the attempt to reach the open roof had failed, and again there was no explanation for Forbis's compulsive drive. Vansittart had first seen him only a month earlier, wandering about blankly on the observation roof of the new administration building at the medical school. How he had gained access to the roof Vansittart had never discovered. Luckily one of the janitors had telephoned him that a man was behaving suspiciously on the roof, and Vansittart had reached him just before the suicide attempt.

At least, that was what it appeared to be. Vansittart examined the little man's placid grey features, his small shoulders and thin hands. There was something anonymous about him. He was minimal urban man, as near a nonentity as possible without friends or family, a vague background of forgotten jobs and rooming houses. The sort of lonely, helpless man who might easily, in an unthinking act of despair, try to throw himself off a roof.

Yet there was something that puzzled Vansittart. Strictly, as a member of the university teaching staff, he should not have prescribed any treatment for Forbis and instead should have handed him over promptly to the police surgeon at the nearest station. But a curious nagging suspicion about Forbis had prevented him from doing so. Later, when he began to analyse Forbis, he found that his personality, or what there was of it, seemed remarkably well integrated, and that he had a realistic, pragmatic approach towards life which was completely unlike the over-compensated self-pity of most would-be suicides.

Nevertheless, he was driven by an insane compulsion, this apparently motiveless impulse to the 100th floor. Despite all Vansittart's probings and tranquillisers Forbis had twice set off for the down-town sector of the city, picked a sky-scraper and trapped himself in his eyrie on the 99th floor, on both occasions finally being rescued by Vansittart.

Deciding to play a hunch, Vansittart asked: "Forbis, have you ever experimented with hypnosis?"

Forbis shifted himself drowsily, then shook his head. "Not as far as I can remember. Are you hinting that someone has given me a post-hypnotic suggestion, trying to make me throw myself off a roof?"

That was quick of you, Vansittart thought. "Why do you say that?" he asked.

"I don't know. But who would try? And what would be

the point?" He peered up at Vansittart. "Do you think someone did?"

Vansittart nodded. "Oh yes. There's no doubt about it." He sat forward, swinging the lamp around for emphasis. "Listen, Forbis, some time ago, I can't be sure how long, three months, perhaps six, someone planted a really powerful post-hypnotic command in your mind. The first part of it— *'Go up to the 100th floor'*—I've been able to uncover, but the rest is still buried. It's that half of the command which worries me. One doesn't need a morbid imagination to guess what it probably is."

Forbis moistened his lips, shielding his eyes from the glare of the lamp. He felt too sluggish to be alarmed by what Vansittart had just said. Despite the doctor's frank admission of failure, and his deliberate but rather nervous manner, he trusted Vansittart, and was confident he would find a solution. "It sounds insane," he commented. "But who would want to kill me? Can't you cancel the whole thing out, erase the command?"

"I've tried to, but without any success. I've been getting nowhere. It's still as strong as ever—stronger, in fact, almost as if it were being reinforced. Where have you been during the last week? Who have you seen?"

Forbis shrugged, sitting up on one elbow. "No-one. As far as I can remember, I've only been on the 99th floor." He searched the air dismally, then gave up. "You know, I can't remember a single thing, just vague outlines of cafes and bus depots, it's strange."

"A pity. I'd try to keep an eye on you, but I can't spare the time. Bauer's retirement hadn't been expected for another year, there's a tremendous amount of reorganisation to be done." He drummed his fingers irritably on the desk. "I notice you've still got some cash with you. Have you had a job?"

"I think so—in the sub-way, perhaps. Or did I just take a train . . . ?" Forbis frowned with the effort of recollection. "I'm sorry, Doctor. Anyway, I've always heard that post-hypnotic suggestions couldn't compel you to do anything that clashed with your basic personality."

"What is the basic personality, though? A skilful analyst can manipulate the psyche to suit the suggestion, magnify a small streak of self-destruction until it cleaves the entire personality like an axe splitting a log."

Forbis pondered this gloomily for a few moments, then brightened slightly. "Well, I seem to have the suggestion beaten. Whatever happens, I can't actually reach the roof, so I must have enough strength to fight it."

Vansittart shook his head. "As a matter of fact, you haven't. It's not you who's keeping yourself off the roof, it's *I*."

"What do you mean?"

"I implanted another hypnotic suggestion, holding you on the 99th floor. When I uncovered the first suggestion I tried to erase it, found I wasn't even scratching the surface, so just as a precaution I inserted a second of my own. '*Get off at the 99th floor.*' How long it will hold you there I don't know, but already it's fading. Today it took you over seven hours to call me. Next time you may get up enough steam to hit the roof. That's why I think we should take a new line, really get to the bottom of this obsession, or rather—" he smiled ruefully "—to the top."

Forbis sat up slowly, massaging his face. "What do you suggest?"

"We'll let you reach the roof. I'll erase my secondary command and we'll see what happens when you step out on to the top deck. Don't worry, I'll be with you if anything goes wrong. It may seem pretty thin consolation, but frankly, Forbis, it would be so easy to kill you and get away with it that I can't understand anyone bothering to go to all this trouble. Obviously there's some deeper motive, something connected, perhaps, with the 100th floor." Vansittart paused, watching Forbis carefully, then asked in a casual voice: "Tell me, have you ever heard of anyone called Fowler?"

He said nothing when Forbis shook his head, but privately noted the reflex pause of unconscious recognition.

"All right?" Vansittart asked as they reached the bottom of the final stairway.

"Fine," Forbis said quietly, catching his breath. He looked up at the rectangular opening above them, wondering how he would feel when he finally reached the roof-top. They had sneaked into the building by one of the service entrances at the rear, and then taken a freight elevator to the 80th floor.

"Let's go, then." Vansittart walked on ahead, beckoning Forbis after him. Together they climbed up to the final doorway, and stepped out into the bright sunlight.

"Doctor . . . !" Forbis exclaimed happily. He felt fresh and exhilarated, his mind clear and unburdened at last. He gazed around the small flat roof, a thousand ideas tumbling past each other in his mind like the crystal fragments of a mountain stream. Somewhere below, however, a deeper current tugged at him.

Go up to the 100*th floor and* . . .

Around him lay the roof-tops of the city, and half a mile away, hidden by the haze, was the spire of the building he had tried to scale the previous day. He strolled about the roof, letting the cool air clear the sweat from his face. There were no suicide grilles around the balcony, but their absence caused him no anxiety.

Vansittart was watching him carefully, black valise in one hand. He nodded encouragingly, then gestured Forbis towards the balcony, eager to rest the valise on the ledge.

"Feel anything?"

"Nothing." Forbis laughed, a brittle chuckle. "It must have been one of those impractical jokes—*'Now let's see you get down.'* Can I look into the street?"

"Of course," Vansittart agreed, bracing himself to seize Forbis if the little man attempted to jump. Beyond the balcony was a thousand-foot drop into a busy shopping thoroughfare.

Forbis clasped the near edge of the balcony in his palms and peered down at the lunch crowds below. Cars edged and shunted like coloured fleas, and people milled about aimlessly on the pavements. Nothing of any interest seemed to be happening.

Beside him, Vansittart frowned and glanced at his watch, wondering whether something had misfired. "It's 12.30," he said. "We'll give you—"

He broke off as footsteps creaked on the stairway below. He swung around and watched the doorway, gesturing to Forbis to keep quiet.

As he turned his back the small man suddenly reached up and cut him sharply across the neck with the edge of his right hand, stunning him momentarily. When Vansittart staggered back he expertly chopped him on both sides of the throat, then sat him down and kicked him senseless with his knees.

Working swiftly, he ignored the broad shadow which reached across the roof to him from the doorway. He carefully fastened Vansittart's three jacket buttons, and then levered him up by the lapels on to his shoulder. Backing against the balcony, he slid him on to the ledge, straightening his legs one after the other. Vansittart stirred helplessly, head lolling from side to side.

And . . . *and* . . .

Behind Forbis the shadow drew nearer, reaching up the side of the balcony, a broad neckless head between heavy shoulders.

Cutting off his pumping breath, Forbis reached out with both hands and pushed.

Ten seconds later, as horns sounded up dimly from the street below, he turned around.

"Good boy, Forbis."

The big man's voice was flat but relaxed. Ten feet from Forbis, he watched him amiably. His face was plump and sallow, a callous mouth half-hidden by a brush moustache. He wore a bulky black overcoat, and one hand rested confidently in a deep pocket.

"Fowler!" Involuntarily, Forbis tried to move forward, for a moment attempting to reassemble his perspectives, but his feet had locked into the white surface of the roof.

Three hundred feet above, an airliner roared over. In a lucid interval provided by the noise, Forbis recognised Fowler, Vansittart's rival for the psychology professorship, remembered the long sessions of hypnosis after Fowler had picked him up in a bar three months earlier, offering to cure his chronic depression before it slid into alcoholism.

With a gasp, he remembered too the rest of the buried command. So Vansittart had been the real target, not himself! *'Go up to the* 100*th floor and* . . .' His first attempt at Vansittart had been a month earlier, when Fowler had left him on the roof and then pretended to be the janitor, but Vansittart had brought two others with him. The mysterious hidden command had been the bait to lure Vansittart to the roof again. Cunningly, Fowler had known that sooner or later Vansittart would yield to the temptation.

"And . . ." he said aloud.

Looking for Vansittart, in the absurd hope that he might have survived the thousand-foot fall, he started for the balcony, then tried to hold himself back as the current caught him.

"*And*—?" Fowler repeated pleasantly. His eyes, two festering points of light, made Forbis sway. "There's still some more to come, isn't there, Forbis? You're beginning to remember it now."

Mind draining, Forbis turned to the balcony, dry mouth sucking at the air.

"*And*—?" Fowler snapped, his voice harder.

. . . *And* . . . *and* . . .

Numbly, Forbis jumped up on to the balcony, and poised on the narrow ledge like a diver, the streets swaying before his eyes. Below, the horns were silent again and the traffic had resumed its flow, a knot of vehicles drawn up in the centre of a small crowd by the edge of the pavement. For a few moments he managed to resist, and then the current caught him, toppling him like a drifting spar.

Fowler stepped quietly through the doorway. Ten seconds later, the horns sounded again.

THIRTEEN TO CENTAURUS

ABEL KNEW.

Three months earlier, just after his sixteenth birthday, he had guessed, but had been too unsure of himself, too overwhelmed by the logic of his discovery, to mention it to his parents. At times, lying back half asleep in his bunk while his mother crooned one of the old lays to herself, he would deliberately repress the knowledge, but always it came back, nagging at him insistently, forcing him to jettison most of what he had long regarded as the real world.

None of the other children at the Station could help. They were immersed in their games in Playroom, or chewing pencils over their tests and homework.

"Abel, what's the matter?" Zenna Peters called after him as he wandered off to the empty store-room on D-Deck. "You're looking sad again."

Abel hesitated, watching Zenna's warm, puzzled smile, then slipped his hands into his pockets and made off, sprinting down the metal stairway to make sure she didn't follow him. Once she sneaked into the store-room uninvited and he had pulled the light-bulb out of the socket, shattered about three weeks of conditioning. Dr. Francis had been furious.

As he hurried along the D-Deck corridor he listened carefully for the doctor, who had recently been keeping an eye on Abel, watching him shrewdly from behind the plastic models in Playroom. Perhaps Abel's mother had told him about the nightmare, when he would wake from a vice of sweating terror, an image of a dull burning disc fixed before his eyes.

If only Dr. Francis could cure him of that dream.

Every six yards down the corridor he stepped through a bulkhead, and idly touched the heavy control boxes on either side of the doorway. Deliberately unfocussing his mind, Abel identified some of the letters above the switches

M-T—R   SC—N

but they scrambled into a blur as soon as he tried to read the

THIRTEEN TO CENTAURUS   13

entire phrase. Conditioning was too strong. After he trapped her in the store-room Zenna had been able to read a few of the notices, but Dr. Francis whisked her away before she could repeat them. Hours later, when she came back, she remembered nothing.

As usual when he entered the store-room, he waited a few seconds before switching on the light, seeing in front of him the small disc of burning light that in his dreams expanded until it filled his brain like a thousand arc lights. It seemed endlessly distant, yet somehow mysteriously potent and magnetic, arousing dormant areas of his mind close to those which responded to his mother's presence.

As the disc began to expand he pressed the switch tab.

To his surprise, the room remained in darkness. He fumbled for the switch, a short cry slipping involuntarily through his lips.

Abruptly, the light went on.

"Hello, Abel," Dr. Francis said easily, right hand pressing the bulb into its socket. "Quite a shock, that one." He leaned against a metal crate. "I thought we'd have a talk together about your essay." He took an exercise book out of his white plastic suit as Abel sat down stiffly. Despite his dry smile and warm eyes there was something about Dr. Francis that always put Abel on his guard.

Perhaps Dr. Francis knew too?

"The Closed Community," Dr. Francis read out. "A strange subject for an essay, Abel."

Abel shrugged. "It was a free choice. Aren't we really expected to choose something unusual?"

Dr. Francis grinned. "A good answer. But seriously, Abel, why pick a subject like that?"

Abel fingered the seals on his suit. These served no useful purpose, but by blowing through them it was possible to inflate the suit. "Well, it's a sort of study of life at the Station, how we all get on with each other. What else is there to write about?—I don't see that it's so strange."

"Perhaps not. No reason why you shouldn't write about the Station. All four of the others did too. But you called yours 'The Closed Community.' The Station isn't closed, Abel—or is it?"

"It's closed in the sense that we can't go outside," Abel explained slowly. "That's all I meant."

"Outside," Dr. Francis repeated. "It's an interesting concept. You must have given the whole subject a lot of thought. When did you first start thinking along these lines?"

"After the dream," Abel said. Dr. Francis had deliberately sidestepped his use of the word 'outside' and he searched for some means of getting to the point. In his pocket he felt the small plumbline he carried around. "Dr. Francis, perhaps you can explain something to me. Why is the Station revolving?"

"Is it?" Dr. Francis looked up with interest. "How do you know?"

Abel reached up and fastened the plumbline to the ceiling stanchion. "The interval between the ball and the wall is about an eighth of an inch greater at the bottom than at the top. Centrifugal forces are driving it outwards. I calculated that the Station is revolving at about two feet per second."

Dr. Francis nodded thoughtfully. "That's just about right," he said matter-of-factly. He stood up. "Let's take a trip to my office. It looks as if it's time you and I had a serious talk."

The Station was on four levels. The lower two contained the crew's quarters, two circular decks of cabins which housed the 14 people on board the Station. The senior clan was the Peters, led by Captain Theodore, a big stern man of taciturn disposition who rarely strayed from Control. Abel had never been allowed there, but the Captain's son, Matthew, often described the hushed dome-like cabin filled with luminous dials and flickering lights, the strange humming music.

All the male members of the Peters clan worked in Control —grandfather Peters, a white-haired old man with humorous eyes, had been Captain before Abel was born—and with the Captain's wife and Zenna they constituted the elite of the Station.

However, the Grangers, the clan to which Abel belonged, was in many respects more important, as he had begun to realize. The day-to-day running of the Station, the detailed programming of emergency drills, duty rosters and commissary menus, was the responsibility of Abel's father, Matthias, and without his firm but flexible hand the Bakers, who cleaned the cabins and ran the commissary, would never have known what to do. And it was only the deliberate intermingling in Recreation which his father devised that brought the Peters and Bakers together, or each family would have stayed indefinitely in its own cabins.

Lastly, there was Dr. Francis. He didn't belong to any of the three clans. Sometimes Abel asked himself where Dr. Francis had come from, but his mind always fogged at a question like that, as the conditioning blocks fell like bulkheads across his thought trains (logic was a dangerous tool at the Station). Dr. Francis' energy and vitality, his relaxed good humor—in a way, he was the only person in the Station who ever made any jokes—were out of character with everyone else. Much as he sometimes disliked Dr. Francis for snooping around and being a know-all, Abel realized how dreary life in the Station would seem without him.

Dr. Francis closed the door of his cabin and gestured Abel into a seat. All the furniture in the Station was bolted to the floor, but Abel noticed that Dr. Francis had unscrewed his chair so that he could tilt it backwards. The hugh vacuum-proof cylinder of the doctor's sleeping tank jutted from the wall, its massive metal body able to withstand any accident the Station might suffer. Abel hated the thought of sleeping in the cylinder—luckily the entire crew quarters were accident-secure—and wondered why Dr. Francis chose to live alone up on A-Deck.

"Tell me, Abel," Dr. Francis began, "has it ever occurred to you to ask why the Station is here?"

Abel shrugged. "Well, it's designed to keep us alive, it's our home."

"Yes, that's true, but obviously it has some other object than just our own survival. Who do you think built the Station in the first place?"

"Our fathers, I suppose, or grandfathers. Or *their* grandfathers."

"Fair enough. And where were they before they built it?"

Abel struggled with the reductio ad absurdum. "I don't know, they must have been floating around in mid-air!"

Dr. Francis joined in the laughter. "Wonderful thought. Actually it's not that far from the truth. But we can't accept that as it stands."

The doctor's self-contained office gave Abel an idea. "Perhaps they came from another Station? An even bigger one?"

Dr. Francis nodded encouragingly. "Brilliant, Abel. A first-class piece of deduction. All right, then, let's assume that. Somewhere, away from us, a hugh Station exists, perhaps a hundred times bigger than this one, maybe even a thousand. Why not?"

"It's possible," Abel admitted, accepting the idea with surprising ease.

"Right. Now you remember your course in advanced mechanics—the imaginary planetary system, with the orbiting bodies held together by mutual gravitational attraction? Let's assume further that such a system actually exists. O.K.?"

"Here?" Abel said quickly. "In your cabin?" Then he added: "In your sleeping cylinder?"

Dr. Francis sat back. "Abel, you do come up with some

amazing things. An interesting association of ideas. No, it would be too big for that. Try to imagine a planetary system orbiting around a central body of absolutely enormous size, each of the planets a million times larger than the Station." When Abel nodded, he went on. "And suppose that the big Station, the one a thousand times larger than this, were attached to one of the planets, and that the people in it decided to go to another planet. So they build a smaller Station, about the size of this one, and send it off through the air. Make sense?"

"In a way." Strangely, the completely abstract concepts were less remote than he would have expected. Deep in his mind dim memories stirred, interlocking with what he had already guessed about the Station. He gazed steadily at Dr. Francis. "You're saying that's what the Station is doing? That the planetary system exists?"

Dr. Francis nodded. "You'd more or less guessed before I told you. Unconsciously, you've known all about it for several years. A few minutes from now I'm going to remove some of the conditioning blocks, and when you wake up in a couple of hours you'll understand everything. You'll know then that in fact the Station is a space ship, flying from our home planet, Earth, where our grandfathers were born, to another planet millions of miles away, in a distant orbiting system. Our grandfathers always lived on Earth, and we are the first people ever to undertake such a journey. You can be proud that you're here. Your grandfather, who volunteered to come, was a great man, and we've got to do everything to make sure that the Station keeps running."

Abel nodded quickly. "When do we get there—the planet we're flying to?"

Dr. Francis looked down at his hands, his face growing sombre. "We'll never get there, Abel. The journey takes too long. This is a multi-generation space vehicle, only our children will land and they'll be old by the time they do. But don't worry, you'll go on thinking of the Station as your only home, and that's deliberate, so that you and your children will be happy here."

He went over to the TV monitor screen by which he kept in touch with Captain Peters, his fingers playing across the control tabs. Suddenly the screen lit up, a blaze of fiery points of light flared into the cabin, throwing a brilliant phosphorescent glitter across the walls, dappling Abel's hands and suit. He gaped at the huge balls of fire, apparently frozen in the middle of a giant explosion, hanging in vast patterns.

"This is the celestial sphere," Dr. Francis explained. "The

star-field into which the Station is moving." He touched a bright speck of light in the lower half of the screen. "Alpha Centauri, the star around which revolves the planet the Station will one day land upon." He turned to Abel. "You remember all these terms I'm using, don't you, Abel? None of them seems strange."

Abel nodded, the wells of his unconscious memory flooding into his mind as Dr. Francis spoke. The TV screen blanked and then revealed a new picture. They appeared to be looking down at an enormous top-like structure, the flanks of a metal pylon sloping towards its center. In the background the star-field rotated slowly in a clockwise direction. "This is the Station," Dr. Francis explained, "seen from a camera mounted on the nose boom. All visual checks have to be made indirectly, as the stellar radiation would blind us. Just below the ship you can see a single star, the Sun, from which we set out 50 years ago. It's now almost too distant to be visible, but a deep inherited memory of it is the burning disc you see in your dreams. We've done what we can to erase it, but unconsciously all of us see it too."

He switched off the set and the brilliant pattern of light swayed and fell back. "The social engineering built into the ship is far more intricate than the mechanical, Abel. It's three generations since the Station set off, and birth, marriage and birth again have followed exactly as they were designed to. As your father's heir great demands are going to be made on your patience and understanding. Any disunity here would bring disaster. The conditioning programs are not equipped to give you more than a general outline of the course to follow. Most of it will be left to you."

"Will you always be here?"

Dr. Francis stood up. "No, Abel, I won't. No one here lives forever. Your father will die, and Captain Peters and myself." He moved to the door. "We'll go now to Conditioning. In three hours' time, when you wake up, you'll find yourself a new man."

Letting himself back into his cabin, Francis leaned wearily against the bulkhead, feeling the heavy rivets with his fingers, here and there flaking away as the metal slowly rusted. When he switched on the TV set he looked tired and dispirited, and gazed absently at the last scene he had shown Abel, the boom camera's view of the ship. He was just about to select another frame when he noticed a dark shadow swing across the surface of the hull.

He leaned forward to examine it, frowning in annoyance as the shadow moved away and faded among the stars. He pressed another tab, and the screen divided into a large chessboard, five frames wide by five deep. The top line showed Control, the main pilot and navigation deck lit by the dim glow of the instrument panels, Captain Peters sitting impassively before the compass screen.

Next, he watched Matthias Granger begin his afternoon inspection of the ship. Most of the passengers seemed reasonably happy, but their faces lacked any lustre. All spent at least 2-3 hours each day bathing in the UV light flooding through the recreation lounge, but the pallor continued, perhaps an unconscious realization that they had been born and were living in what would also be their own tomb. Without the continuous conditioning sessions, and the hypnotic reassurance of the sub-sonic voices, they would long ago have become will-less automatons.

Switching off the set, he prepared to climb into the sleeping cylinder. The airlock was three feet in diameter, waist-high off the floor. The time seal rested at zero, and he moved it forward 12 hours, then set it so that the seal could only be broken from within. He swung the lock out and crawled in over the moulded foam mattress, snapping the door shut behind him.

Lying back in the thin yellow light, he slipped his fingers through the ventilator grille in the rear wall, pressed the unit into its socket and turned it sharply. Somewhere an electric motor throbbed briefly, the end wall of the cylinder swung back slowly like a vault door and bright daylight poured in.

Quickly, Francis climbed out onto a small metal platform that jutted from the upper slope of a huge white asbestos-covered dome. Fifty feet above was the roof of a large hangar. A maze of pipes and cables traversed the surface of the dome, interlacing like the vessels of a giant bloodshot eye, and a narrow stairway led down to the floor below. The entire dome, some 150 feet wide, was revolving slowly. A line of five trucks was drawn up by the stores depot on the far side of the hangar, and a man in a brown uniform waved to him from one of the glass-walled offices.

At the bottom of the ladder he jumped down onto the hangar floor, ignoring the curious stares from the soldiers unloading the stores. Half-way across he craned up at the revolving bulk of the dome. A black perforated sail, 50 feet square, like a fragment of a planetarium, was suspended from the roof over the apex of the dome, a TV camera directly below it, a large metal sphere mounted about five feet from the lens. One of the guy-ropes had snapped and the sail tilted slightly to reveal the catwalk along the center of the roof.

He pointed this out to a maintenance sergeant warming his hands in one of the ventilator outlets from the dome. "You'll have to string that back. Some fool was wandering along the catwalk and throwing his shadow straight onto the model. I could see it clearly on the TV screen. Luckily no one spotted it."

"O.K., Doctor, I'll get it fixed." He chuckled sourly. "That would have been a laugh, though. Really give them something to worry about."

The man's tone annoyed Francis. "They've got plenty to worry about as it is."

"I don't know about that, Doctor. Some people here think they have it all ways. Quiet and warm in there, nothing to do except sit back and listen to those hypno-drills." He looked out bleakly at the abandoned airfield stretching away to the cold tundra beyond the perimeter, and turned up his collar. "We're the boys back here on Mother Earth who do the work, out in this Godforsaken dump. If you need any more space cadets, Doctor, remember me."

Francis managed a smile and stepped into the control office, made his way through the clerks sitting at trestle tables in front of the progress charts. Each carried the name of one of the dome passengers and a tabulated breakdown of progress through the psychometric tests and conditioning programs. Other charts listed the day's rosters, copies of those posted that morning by Matthias Granger.

Inside Colonel Chalmers' office Francis relaxed back gratefully in the warmth, describing the salient features of his day's observation. "I wish you could go in there and move around them, Paul," he concluded, "it's not the same spying through the TV cameras. You've got to talk to them, measure yourself against people like Granger and Peters."

"You're right, they're fine men, like all the others. It's a pity they're wasted there."

"They're not wasted," Francis insisted. "Every piece of data will be immensely valuable when the first space ships set out." He ignored Chalmers' muttered 'If they do' and went on: "Zenna and Abel worry me a little. It may be necessary to bring forward the date of their marriage. I know it will raise eyebrows, but the girl is as fully mature at 15 as she will be four years from now, and she'll be a settling influence on Abel, stop him from thinking too much."

Chalmers shook his head doubtfully. "Sounds a good

idea, but a girl of 15 and a boy of 16—? You'd raise a
storm, Roger. Technically they're wards of court, every
decency league would be up in arms."

Francis gestured irritably. "Need they know? We've really
got a problem with Abel, the boy's too clever. He'd more
or less worked out for himself that the Station was a space
ship, he merely lacked the vocabulary to describe it. Now
that we're starting to lift the conditioning blocks he'll want
to know everything. It will be a big job to prevent him from
smelling a rat, particularly with the slack way this place
is being run. Did you see the shadow on the TV screen?
We're damn lucky Peters didn't have a heart attack."

Chalmers nodded. "I'm getting that tightened up. A few
mistakes are bound to happen, Roger. It's damn cold for
the control crew working around the dome. Try to remember that the people outside are just as important as those
inside."

"Of course. The real trouble is that the budget is ludi-
crously out of date. It's only been revised once in 50 years.
Perhaps General Short can generate some official interest,
get a new deal for us. He sounds like a pretty brisk new
broom." Chalmers pursed his lips doubtfully, but Francis
continued: "I don't know whether the tapes are wearing out,
but the negative conditioning doesn't hold as well as it used
to. We'll probably have to tighten up the programs. I've
made a start by pushing Abel's graduation forward."

"Yes, I watched you on the screen here. The control boys
became quite worked up next door. One or two of them are
as keen as you, Roger, they'd been programming ahead
for three months. It meant a lot of time wasted for them.
I think you ought to check with me before you make a
decision like that. The dome isn't your private laboratory."

Francis accepted the reproof. Lamely, he said: "It was
one of those spot decisions, I'm sorry. There was nothing
else to do."

Chalmers gently pressed home his point. "I'm not so sure.
I thought you rather overdid the long-term aspects of the
journey. Why go out of your way to tell him he would never
reach planet-fall? It only heightens his sense of isolation,
makes it that much more difficult if we decide to shorten
the journey."

Francis looked up. "There's no chance of that, is there?"

Chalmers paused thoughtfully. "Roger, I really advise you
not to get too involved with the project. Keep saying to
yourself: they're-not-going-to-Alpha-Centauri. They're here on
Earth, and if the government decided it they'd be let out

tomorrow. I know the courts would have to sanction it but that's a formality. It's 50 years since this project was started and a good number of influential people feel that it's gone on for too long. Ever since the Mars and Moon colonies failed space programs have been cut right back. They think the money here is being poured away for the amusement of a few sadistic psychologists."

"You know that isn't true," Francis retorted. "I may have been over-hasty, but on the whole this project has been scrupulously conducted. Without exaggeration, if you did send a dozen people on a multi-generation ship to Alpha Centauri you couldn't do better than duplicate everything that's taken place here, down to the last cough and sneeze. If the information we've obtained had been available the Mars and Moon colonies never would have failed!"

"True. But irrelevant. Don't you understand, when everyone was eager to get into space they were prepared to accept the idea of a small group being sealed into a tank for 100 years, particularly when the original team volunteered. Now, when interest has evaporated, people are beginning to feel that there's something obscene about this human zoo, what began as a grand adventure of the spirit of Columbus has become a grisly joke. In one sense we've learned too much—the social stratification of the three families is the sort of unwelcome datum that doesn't do the project much good. Another is the complete ease with which we've manipulated them, made them believe anything we've wanted." Chalmers leaned forward across the desk. "Confidentially, Roger, General Short has been put in command for one reason only—to close this place down. It may take years, but it's going to be done, I warn you. The important job now is to get those people out of there, not keep them in."

Francis stared bleakly at Chalmers. "Do you really believe that?"

"Frankly, Roger, yes. This project should never have been launched. You can't manipulate people the way we're doing—the endless hyno-drills, the forced pairing of children —look at yourself, five minutes ago you were seriously thinking of marrying two teen-age children just to stop them using their minds. The whole thing degrades human dignity, all the taboos, the increasing degree of introspection—sometimes Peters and Granger don't speak to anyone for two or three weeks—the way life in the dome has become tenable only by accepting the insane situation as the normal one. I think the reaction against the project is healthy."

Francis stared out at the dome. A gang of men were loading the so-called 'compressed food' (actually frozen foods with the brand names removed) into the commissary hatchway. Next morning, when Baker and his wife dialled the pre-arranged menu, the supplies would be promptly delivered, apparently from the space-hold. To some people, Francis knew, the project might well seem a complete fraud.

Quietly he said: "The people who volunteered accepted the sacrifice, and all it involved. How's Short going to get them out? Just open the door and whistle?"

Chalmers smiled, a little wearily. "He's not a fool, Roger. He's as sincerely concerned about their welfare as you are. Half the crew, particularly the older ones, would go mad within five minutes. But don't be disappointed, the project has more than proved its worth."

"It won't do that until they 'land'. If the project ends it will be we who have failed, not them. We can't rationalize by saying it's cruel or unpleasant. We owe it to the 14 people in the dome to keep it going."

Chalmers watched him shrewdly. "14? You mean 13, don't you, Doctor? Or are you inside the dome too?"

The ship had stopped rotating. Sitting at his desk in Command, planning the next day's fire drills, Abel noticed the sudden absence of movement. All morning, as he walked around the ship—he no longer used the term Station—he had been aware of an inward drag that pulled him towards the wall, as if one leg were shorter than the other.

When he mentioned this to his father the older man merely said: "Captain Peters is in charge of Control. Always let him worry where the navigation of the ship is concerned."

This sort of advice now meant nothing to Abel. In the previous two months his mind had attacked everything around him voraciously, probing and analyzing, examining every facet of life in the Station. An enormous, once suppressed vocabulary of abstract terms and relationships lay latent below the surface of his mind, and nothing would stop him applying it.

Over their meal trays in the commissary he grilled Matthew Peters about the ship's flight path, the great parabola which would carry it to Alpha Centauri.

"What about the currents built into the ship?" he asked. "The rotation was designed to eliminate the magnetic poles set up when the ship was originally constructed. How are you compensating for that?"

Matthew looked puzzled. "I'm not sure, exactly. Probably the instruments are automatically compensated." When Abel smiled skeptically he shrugged. "Anyway, Father knows all about it. There's no doubt we're right on course."

"We hope," Abel murmured sotto voce. The more Abel asked Matthew about the navigational devices he and his father operated in Control the more obvious it became that they were merely carrying out low-level instrument checks, and that their role was limited to replacing burnt-out pilot lights. Most of the instruments operated automatically, and they might as well have been staring at cabinets full of mattress floc.

What a joke if they were!

Smiling to himself, Abel realized that he had probably stated no more than the truth. It would be unlikely for the navigation to be entrusted to the crew when the slightest human error could throw the space ship irretrievably out of control, send it hurtling into a passing star. The designers of the ship would have sealed the automatic pilots well out of reach, given the crew light supervisory duties that created an illusion of control.

That was the real clue to life aboard the ship. None of their roles could be taken at face value. The day-to-day, minute-to-minute programming carried out by himself and his father were merely a set of variations on a pattern already laid down; the permutations possible were endless, but the fact that he could send Matthew Peters to the commissary at 12 o'clock rather than 12:30 didn't give him any real power over Matthew's life. The master programs printed by the computers selected the day's menus, safety drills and recreation periods, and a list of names to choose from, but the slight leeway allowed, the extra two or three names supplied, were there in case of illness, not to give Abel any true freedom of choice.

One day, Abel promised himself, he would program himself out of the conditioning sessions. Shrewdly he guessed that the conditioning still blocked out a great deal of interesting material, that half his mind remained submerged. Something about the ship suggested that there might be more to it than—

"Hello, Abel, you look far away." Dr. Francis sat down next to him. "What's worrying you?"

"I was just calculating something," Abel explained quickly. "Tell me, assuming that each member of the crew consumes about three pounds of non-circulated food each day, roughly half a ton per year, the total cargo must be about 800 tons, and that's not allowing for any supplies after planet-fall. There should be at least 1500 tons aboard. Quite a weight."

"Not in absolute terms, Abel. The Station is only a small fraction of the ship. The main reactors, fuel tanks and space holds together weigh over 30,000 tons. They provide the gravitational pull that holds you to the floor."

Abel shook his head slowly. "Hardly, Doctor, the attraction must come from the stellar gravitational fields, or the weight of the ship would have to be about 6×10^{20} tons."

Dr. Francis watched Abel reflectively, aware that the young man had led him into a simple trap. The figure he had quoted was near enough the Earth's mass. "These are complex problems, Abel. I wouldn't worry too much about stellar mechanics. Captain Peters has that responsibility."

"I'm not trying to usurp it," Abel assured him. "Merely to extend my own knowledge. Don't you think it might be worth departing from the rules a little? For example, it would be interesting to test the effects of continued isolation. We could select a small group, subject them to artificial stimuli, even seal them off from the rest of the crew and condition them to believe they were back on Earth. It could be a really valuable experiment, Doctor."

As he waited in the conference room for General Short to finish his opening harangue, Francis repeated the last sentence to himself, wondering idly what Abel, with his limitless enthusiasm, would have made of the circle of defeated faces around the table.

". . . regret as much as you do, gentlemen, the need to discontinue the project. However, now that a decision has been made by the Space Department, it is our duty to implement it. Of course, the task won't be an easy one. What we need is a phased withdrawal, a gradual readjustment of the world around the crew that will bring them down to Earth as gently as a parachute." The General was a brisk, sharp-faced man in his fifties, with burly shoulders but sensitive eyes. He turned to Dr. Kersh, who was responsible for the dietary and biometric controls aboard the dome. "From what you tell me, Doctor, we might not have as much time as we'd like. This boy Abel sounds something of a problem."

Kersh smiled. "I was looking in at the commissary, overheard him tell Dr. Francis that he wanted to run an experiment on a small group of the crew. An isolation drill, would you believe it. He's estimated that the two-man tractor crews may be isolated for up to two years when the first foraging trips are made."

Captain Sanger, the engineering officer, added: "He's also trying to duck his conditioning sessions. He's wearing a couple of foam pads under his earphones, missing about

90% of the sub-sonics. We spotted it when the EEG tape we record showed no alpha waves. At first we thought it was a break in the cable, but when we checked visually on the screen we saw that he had his eyes open. He wasn't listening."

Francis drummed on the table. "It wouldn't have mattered. The sub-sonic was a maths instruction sequence—the four-figure antilog system."

"A good thing he did miss them," Kersh said with a laugh. "Sooner or later he'll work out that the dome is travelling in an elliptical orbit 93 million miles from a dwarf star of the G_0 spectral class."

"What are you doing about this attempt to evade conditioning, Dr. Francis?" Short asked. When Francis shrugged vaguely he added: "I think we ought to regard the matter fairly seriously. From now on we'll be relying on the programming."

Flatly, Francis said: "Abel will resume the conditioning. There's no need to do anything. Without the regular daily contact he'll soon feel lost. The sub-sonic voice is composed of his mother's vocal tones, when he no longer hears it he'll lose his orientations, feel completely deserted."

Short nodded slowly. "Well, let's hope so." He addressed Dr. Kersh. "At a rough estimate, Doctor, how long will it take to bring them back? Bearing in mind they'll have to be given complete freedom and that every TV and newspaper network in the world will interview each one a hundred times."

Kersh chose his words carefully. "Obviously a matter of years, General. All the conditioning drills will have to be gradually re-scored, as a stop-gap measure we may need to introduce a meteor collision . . . guessing, I'd say three to five years. Possibly longer."

"Fair enough. What would you estimate, Dr. Francis?"

Francis fiddled with his blotter, trying to view the question seriously. "I've no idea. *Bring them back*. What do you really mean, General? Bring what back?" Irritated, he snapped: "A hundred years."

Laughter crossed the table, and Short smiled at him, not unamiably. "That's fifty years more than the original project, Doctor. You can't have been doing a very good job here."

Francis shook his head. "You're wrong, General. The original project was to get them to Alpha Centauri. Nothing was said about bringing them *back*." When the laughter fell away Francis cursed himself for his foolishness; antagonizing the General wouldn't help the people in the dome.

But Short seemed unruffled. "All right, then, it's obviously going to take some time." Pointedly, with a glance at Francis, he added: "It's the men and women in the ship we're thinking of, not ourselves, if we need a hundred years we'll take them, not one less. You may be interested to hear that the Space Department chiefs feel about fifteen years will be necessary. At least." There was a quickening of interest around the table. Francis watched Short with surprise. In fifteen years a lot could happen, there might be another spaceward swing of public opinion.

"The Department recommends that the project continue as before, with whatever budgetary parings we can make—stopping the dome is just a start—and that we condition the crew to believe that a round trip is in progress, that their mission is merely one of reconnaissance, and that they are bringing vital information back to Earth. When they step out of the space-ship they'll be treated as heroes and accept the strangeness of the world around them." Short looked across the table, waiting for someone to reply. Kersh stared doubtfully at his hands, and Sanger and Chalmers played mechanically with their blotters.

Just before Short continued Francis pulled himself together, realizing that he was faced with his last opportunity to save the project. However much they disagreed with Short, none of the others would try to argue with him.

"I'm afraid that won't do, General," he said, "though I appreciate the Department's foresight and your own sympathetic approach. The scheme you've outlined sounds plausible, but it just won't work." He sat forward, his voice controlled and precise. "General, ever since they were children these people have been trained to accept that they were a closed group, and would never have contact with anyone else. On the unconscious level, on the level of their functional nervous systems, no one else in the world exists, for them the neuronic basis of reality is isolation. You'll never train them to invert their whole universe, any more than you can train a fish to fly. If you start to tamper with the fundamental patterns of their psyches you'll produce the sort of complete mental block you see when you try to teach a left-handed person to use his right."

Francis glanced at Dr. Kersh, who was nodding in agreement. "Believe me, General, contrary to what you and the Space Department naturally assume, the people in the dome do *not* want to come out. Given the choice they would prefer to stay there, just as the gold-fish prefers to stay in its bowl."

Short paused before replying, evidently re-assessing Francis. "You may be right, Doctor," he admitted. "But where does that get us? We've got 15 years, perhaps 25 at the outside."

"There's only one way to do it," Francis told him. "Let the project continue, exactly as before, but with one difference. Prevent them from marrying and having children. In 25 years only the present younger generation will still be alive, and a further five years from then they'll all be dead. A life span in the dome is little more than 45 years. At the age of 30 Abel will probably be an old man. When they start to die off no one will care about them any longer."

There was a full half minute's silence, and then Kersh said: "It's the best suggestion, General. Humane, and yet faithful both to the original project and the Department's instructions. The absence of children would be only a slight deviation from the conditioned pathway. The basic isolation of the group would be strengthened, rather than diminished, also their realization that they themselves will never see planet-fall. If we drop the pedagogical drills and play down the space flight they will soon become a small closed community, little different from any other out-group on the road to extinction."

Chalmers cut in: "Another point, General. It would be far easier—and cheaper—to stage, and as the members died off we could progressively close down the ship until finally there might be only a single deck left, perhaps even a few cabins."

Short stood up and paced over to the window, looking out through the clear glass over the frosted panes at the great dome in the hangar.

"It sounds a dreadful prospect," he commented. "Completely insane. As you say, though, it may be the only way out."

Moving quietly among the trucks parked in the darkened hangar, Francis paused for a moment to look back at the lighted windows of the control deck. Two or three of the night staff sat watch over the line of TV screens, half asleep themselves as they observed the sleeping occupants of the dome.

He ducked out of the shadows and ran across to the dome, climbed the stairway to the entrance point thirty feet above. Opening the external lock, he crawled in and closed it behind him, then unfastened the internal entry hatch and pulled himself out of the sleeping cylinder into the silent cabin.

A single dim light glowed over the TV monitor screen as it

revealed the three orderlies in the control deck, lounging back in a haze of cigarette smoke six feet from the camera.

Francis turned up the speaker volume, then tapped the mouthpiece sharply with his knuckle.

Tunic unbuttoned, sleep still shadowing his eyes, Colonel Chalmers leaned forward intently into the screen, the orderlies at his shoulder.

"Believe me, Roger, you're proving nothing. General Short and the Space Department won't withdraw their decision now that a special bill of enactment has been passed." When Francis still looked skeptical he added: "If anything, you're more likely to jeopardize them."

"I'll take a chance," Francis said. "Too many guarantees have been broken in the past. Here I'll be able to keep an eye on things." He tried to sound cool and unemotional; the cine-cameras would be recording the scene and it was important to establish the right impression. General Short would be only too keen to avoid a scandal. If he decided Francis was unlikely to sabotage the project he would probably leave him in the dome.

Chalmers pulled up a chair, his face earnest, "Roger, give yourself time to reconsider everything. You may be more of a discordant element than you realize. Remember, nothing would be easier than getting you out—a child could cut his way through the rusty hull with a blunt can-opener."

"Don't try it," Francis warned him quietly. "I'll be moving down to C-Deck, so if you come in after me they'll all know. Believe me, I won't try to interfere with the withdrawal programs. And I won't arrange any teen-age marriages. But I think the people inside may need me now for more than eight hours a day."

"Francis!" Chalmers shouted. "Once you go down there you'll never come out! Don't you realize you're entombing yourself in a situation that's totally unreal? You're deliberately withdrawing into a nightmare, sending yourself off on a non-stop journey to *nowhere!*"

Curtly, before he switched the set off for the last time, Francis replied: "Not nowhere, Colonel—Alpha Centauri."

Sitting down thankfully in the narrow bunk in his cabin, Francis rested briefly before setting off for the commissary. All day he had been busy coding the computer punch tapes for Abel, and his eyes ached with the strain of manually stamping each one of the thousands of minuscule holes. For eight hours he had sat without a break in the small isolation cell, electrodes clamped to his chest, knees and elbows while Abel measured his cardiac and respiratory rhythms.

The tests bore no relation to the daily programs Abel now worked out for his father, and Francis was finding it difficult to maintain his patience. Initially Abel had tested his ability to follow a prescribed set of instructions, producing an endless exponential function, then a digital representation of *pi* to a thousand places. Finally Abel had persuaded Francis to cooperate in a more difficult test—the task of producing a totally random sequence. Whenever he unconsciously repeated a simple progression, as he did if he was tired or bored, or a fragment of a larger possible progression, the computer scanning his progress sounded an alarm on the desk and he would have to start afresh. After a few hours the buzzer rasped out every ten seconds, snapping at him like a bad-tempered insect. Francis had finally hobbled over to the door that afternoon, entangling himself in the electrode leads, found to his annoyance that the door was locked (ostensibly to prevent any interruption by a fire patrol), then saw through the small porthole that the computer in the cubicle outside was running unattended.

But when Francis' pounding roused Abel from the far end of the next laboratory he had been almost irritable with the doctor for wanting to discontinue the experiment.

"Damn it, Abel, I've been punching away at these things for three weeks now." He winced as Abel disconnected him, brusquely tearing off the adhesive tape. "Trying to produce random sequences isn't all that easy—my sense of reality is beginning to fog." (Sometimes he wondered if Abel was secretly waiting for this.) "I think I'm entitled to a vote of thanks."

"But we arranged for the trial to last three days, Doctor," Abel pointed out. "It's only later that the valuable results begin to appear. It's the errors you make that are interesting. The whole experiment is pointless now."

"Well, it's probably pointless anyway. Some mathematicians used to maintain that a random sequence was impossible to define."

"But we can assume that it *is* possible," Abel insisted. "I was just giving you some practice before we started on the trans-finite numbers."

Francis baulked here. "I'm sorry, Abel. Maybe I'm not so fit as I used to be. Anyway, I've got other duties to attend to."

"But they don't take long, Doctor. There's really nothing for you to do now."

He was right, as Francis was forced to admit. In the year he had spent in the dome Abel had remarkably streamlined the daily routines, provided himself and Francis with an excess of leisure time, particularly as the latter never went to conditioning (Francis was frightened of the sub-sonic vocies—Chalmers and Short would be subtle in their attempts to extricate him, perhaps too subtle).

Life aboard the dome had been more of a drain on him than he anticipated. Chained to the routines of the ship, limited in his recreations and with few intellectual pastimes— there were no books aboard the ship—he found it increasingly difficult to sustain his former good humor, was beginning to sink into the deadening lethargy that had overcome most of the other crew members. Matthias Granger had retreated to his cabin, content to leave the programming to Abel, spent his time playing with a damaged clock, while the two Peters rarely strayed from Control. The three wives were almost completely inert, satisfied to knit and murmur to each other. The days passed indistinguishably. Sometimes, Francis told himself wryly, he nearly *did* believe that they were en route for Alpha Centauri. That would have been a joke for General Short!

At 6:30, when he went to the commissary for his evening meal, he found that he was a quarter of an hour late.

"Your meal time was changed this afternoon," Baker told him, lowering the hatchway. "I got nothing ready for you."

Francis began to remonstrate but the man was adamant. "I can't make a special dip into space-hold just because you didn't look at Routine Orders, can I, Doctor?"

On the way out Francis met Abel, tried to persuade him to countermand the order. "You could have warned me, Abel. Damnation, I've been sitting inside your test rig all afternoon."

"But you went back to your cabin, Doctor," Abel pointed out smoothly. "You pass three SRO bulletins on your way from the laboratory. Always look at them at every opportunity, remember. Last-minute changes are liable at any time. I'm afraid you'll have to wait until 10:30 now."

Francis went back to his cabin, suspecting that the sudden change had been Abel's revenge on him for discontinuing the test. He would have to be more conciliatory with Abel, or the young man could make his life a hell, literally starve him to death. Escape from the dome was impossible now —there was a mandatory 20-year sentence on anyone making an unauthorized entry into the space simulator.

After resting for an hour or so, he left his cabin at 8 o'clock to carry out his duty checks of the pressure seals by the B-Deck Meteor Screen. He always went through the pretense of reading them, enjoying the sense of participation in the space flight which the exercise gave him, deliberately accepting the illusion.

The seals were mounted in the control points at ten-yard intervals along the perimeter corridor, a narrow circular passageway around the main corridor. Alone there, the servos clicking and snapping, he felt at peace within the space vehicle. "Earth itself is in orbit around the Sun," he mused as he checked the seals, "and the whole solar system is travelling at 40 miles a second towards the constellation Lyra. The degree of illusion that exists is a complex question."

Something cut through his reverie.

The pressure indicator was flickering slightly. The needle wavered between 0.001 and 0.0015 psi. The pressure inside the dome was fractionally above atmospheric, in order that dust might be expelled through untoward cracks (though the main object of the pressure seals was to get the crew safely into the vacuum-proof emergency cylinders in case the dome was damaged and required internal repairs).

For a moment Francis panicked, wondering whether Short had decided to come in after him—the reading, although meaningless, indicated that a breach had opened in the hull. Then the hand moved back to zero, and footsteps sounded along the radial corridor at right angles past the next bulkhead.

Quickly Francis stepped into its shadow. Before his death old Peters had spent a lot of time mysteriously pottering around the corridor, probably secreting a private food cache behind one of the rusting panels.

He leaned forward as the footsteps crossed the corridor. Abel?

He watched the young man disappear down a stairway, then made his way into the radial corridor, searching the steel-grey sheeting for a retractable panel. Immediately adjacent to the end wall of the corridor, against the outer skin of the dome, was a small fire control booth.

A tuft of slate-white hairs lay on the floor of the booth. Asbestos fibres!

Francis stepped into the booth, within a few seconds located a loosened panel that had rusted off its rivets. About ten inches by six, it slid back easily. Beyond it was the outer wall of the dome, a hand's breadth away. Here too was a loose plate, held in position by a crudely fashioned hook.

Francis hesitated, then lifted the hook and drew back the panel.

He was looking straight down into the hangar!

Below, a line of trucks was disgorging supplies onto the concrete floor under a couple of spotlights, a sergeant shouting orders at the labor squad. To the right was the control deck, Chalmers in his office on the evening shift.

The spy-hole was directly below the stairway, and the overhanging metal steps shielded it from the men in the hangar. The asbestos had been carefully frayed so that it concealed the retractable plate. The wire hook was as badly rusted as the rest of the hull, and Francis estimated that the window had been in use for over 30 or 40 years.

So almost certainly old Peters had regularly looked out through the window, and knew perfectly well that the space ship was a myth. Nonetheless he had stayed aboard, perhaps realizing that the truth would destroy the others, or preferred to be captain of an artificial ship rather than a self-exposed curiosity in the world outside.

Presumably he had passed on the secret. Not to his bleak taciturn son, but to the one other lively mind, one who would keep the secret and make the most of it. For his own reasons he too had decided to stay in the dome, realizing that he would soon be the effective captain, free to pursue his experiments in applied psychology. He might even have failed to grasp that Francis was not a true member of the crew. His confident mastery of the programming, his lapse of interest in Control, his casualness over the safety devices, all meant one thing—

Abel knew!

TRACK 12

"GUESS AGAIN," Sheringham said.

Maxted clipped on the headphones, carefully settled them over his ears. He concentrated as the disc began to spin, trying to catch some echo of identity.

The sound was a rapid metallic rustling, like iron filings splashing through a funnel. It ran for ten seconds, repeated itself a dozen times, then ended abruptly in a string of blips.

"Well?" Sheringham asked. "What is it?"

Maxted pulled off his headphones, rubbed one of his ears.

He had been listening to the records for hours and his ears felt bruised and numb.

"Could be anything. An ice-cube melting?"

Sheringham shook his head, his little beard wagging.

Maxted shrugged. "A couple of galaxies colliding?"

"No. Sound waves don't travel through space. I'll give you a clue. It's one of those *proverbial* sounds." He seemed to be enjoying the catechism.

Maxted lit a cigarette, threw the match onto the laboratory bench. The head melted a tiny pool of wax, froze and left a shallow black scar. He watched it pleasurably, conscious of Sheringham fidgeting beside him.

He pumped his brains for an obscene simile. "What about a fly—"

"Time's up," Sheringham cut in. *"A pin dropping."* He took the 3-inch disc off the player, angled it into its sleeve. "In actual fall, that is, not impact. We used a fifty-foot shaft and eight microphones. I thought you'd get that one."

He reached for the last record, a 12-inch LP, but Maxted stood up before he got it to the turntable. Through the french windows he could see the patio, a table, glasses and decanter gleaming in the darkness. Sheringham and his infantile games suddenly irritated him; he felt impatient with himself for tolerating the man so long.

"Let's get some air," he said brusquely, shouldering past one of the amplifier rigs. "My ears feel like gongs."

"By all means," Sheringham agreed promptly. He placed the record carefully on the turntable and switched off the player. "I want to save this one until later, anyway."

They went out into the warm evening air. Sheringham turned on the japanese lanterns and they stretched back in the wicker chairs under the open sky.

"I hope you weren't too bored," Sheringham said as he handled the decanter. "Microsonics is a fascinating hobby, but I'm afraid I may have let it become an obsession."

Maxted grunted non-committally. "Some of the records are interesting," he admitted. "They have a sort of crazy novelty value, like blown-up photographs of moths' faces and razor blades. Despite what you claim, though, I can't believe microsonics will ever become a scientific tool. It's just an elaborate laboratory toy."

Sheringham shook his head. "You're completely wrong, of course. Remember the cell division series I played first of all? Amplified 100,000 times animal cell division sounds like a lot of girders and steel sheets being ripped apart—how did you put it?—a car smash in slow motion. On the other hand, plant cell division is an electronic poem, all soft chords and bubbling tones. Now there you have a perfect illustration of how microsonics can reveal the distinction between the animal and plant kingdoms."

"Seems a damned roundabout way of doing it," Maxted commented, helping himself to soda. "You might as well calculate the speed of your car from the apparent motion of the stars. Possible, but it's easier to look at the speedometer."

Sheringham nodded, watching Maxted closely across the table. His interest in the conversation appeared to have exhausted itself, and the two men sat silently with their glasses. Strangely, the hostility between them, of so many years' standing, now became less veiled, the contrast of personality, manner and physique more pronounced. Maxted, a tall fleshy man with a coarse handsome face, lounged back almost horizontally in his chair, thinking about Susan Sheringham. She was at the Turnbull's party, and but for the fact that it was no longer discreet of him to be seen at the Turnbull's— for the all-too-familiar reason—he would have passed the evening with her, rather than with her grotesque little husband.

He surveyed Sheringham with as much detachment as he could muster, wondering whether this prim unattractive man, with his pedantry and in-bred academic humour, had any redeeming qualities whatever. None, certainly, at a casual glance, though it required some courage and pride to have invited him round that evening. His motives, however, would be typically eccentric.

The pretext, Maxted reflected, had been slight enough— Sheringham, professor of biochemistry at the university, maintained a lavish home laboratory; Maxted, a run-down athlete with a bad degree, acted as torpedo-man for a company manufacturing electron microscopes; a visit, Sheringham had suggested over the phone, might be to the profit of both.

Of course, nothing of this had in fact been mentioned. But nor, as yet, had he referred to Susan, the real subject of the evening's charade. Maxted speculated upon the possible routes Sheringham might take toward the inevitable confrontation scene; not for him the nervous circular pacing, the well-thumbed photostat, or the thug at the shoulder. There was a vicious adolescent streak running through Sheringham—

Maxted broke out of his reverie abruptly. The air in the patio had become suddenly cooler, almost as if a powerful refrigerating unit had been switched on. A rash of goose-flesh raced up his thighs and down the back of his neck, and he reached forward and finished what was left of his whisky.

"Cold out here," he commented.

Sheringham glanced at his watch. "Is it?" he said. There was a hint of indecision in his voice; for a moment he seemed to be waiting for a signal. Then he pulled himself together and, with an odd half-smile, said: "Time for the last record."

"What do you mean?" Maxted asked.

"Don't move," Sheringham said. He stood up. "I'll put it on." He pointed to a loudspeaker screwed to the wall above Maxted's head, grinned and ducked out.

Shivering uncomfortably, Maxted peered up into the silent evening sky, hoping that the vertical current of cold air that had sliced down into the patio would soon dissipate itself.

A low noise crackled from the speaker, multiplied by a circle of other speakers which he noticed for the first time had been slung among the trellis-work around the patio.

Shaking his head sadly at Sheringham's antics, he decided to help himself to more whisky. As he stretched across the table he swayed and rolled back uncontrollably into his chair. His stomach seemed to be full of mercury, ice-cold and enormously heavy. He pushed himself forward again, trying to reach the glass, and knocked it across the table. His brain began to fade, and he leaned his elbows helplessly on the glass edge of the table and felt his head fall onto his wrists.

When he looked up again Sheringham was standing in front of him, smiling sympathetically.

"Not too good, eh?" he said.

Breathing with difficulty, Maxted managed to lean back. He tried to speak to Sheringham, but he could no longer remember any words. His heart switchbacked, and he grimaced at the pain.

"Don't worry," Sheringham assured him. "The fibrillation is only a side effect. Disconcerting, perhaps, but it will soon pass."

He strolled leisurely around the patio, scrutinizing Maxted from several angles. Evidently satisfied, he sat down on the table. He picked up the siphon and swirled the contents about. "Chromium cyanate. Inhibits the coenzyme system controlling the body's fluid balances, floods hydroxyl ions into the bloodstream. In brief, you drown. Really drown, that is, not merely suffocate as you would if you were immersed in an external bath. However, I mustn't distract you."

He inclined his head at the speakers. Being fed into the patio was a curiously muffled spongy noise, like elastic waves lapping in a latex sea. The rhythms were huge and ungainly, overlayed by the deep leaden wheezing of a gigantic bellows. Barely audible at first, the sounds rose until they filled the patio and shut out the few traffic noises along the highway.

"Fantastic, isn't it?" Sheringham said. Twirling the siphon

by its neck he stepped over Maxted's legs and adjusted the tone control under one of the speaker boxes. He looked blithe and spruce, almost ten years younger. "These are 30-second repeats, 400 microsens, amplification one thousand. I admit I've edited the track a little, but it's still remarkable how repulsive a beautiful sound can become. You'll never guess what this was."

Maxted stirred sluggishly. The lake of mercury in his stomach was as cold and bottomless as an oceanic trench, and his arms and legs had become enormous, like the bloated appendages of a drowned giant. He could just see Sheringham bobbing about in front of him, and hear the slow beating of the sea in the distance. Nearer now, it pounded with a dull insistent rhythm, the great waves ballooning and bursting like bubbles in a lava sea.

"I'll tell you, Maxted, it took me a year to get that recording," Sheringham was saying. He straddled Maxted, gesturing with the siphon. "A year. Do you know how ugly a year can be?" For a moment he paused, then tore himself from the memory. "Last Saturday, just after midnight, you and Susan were lying back in this same chair. You know, Maxted, there are audio-probes everywhere here. Slim as pencils, with a six-inch focus. I had four in that headrest alone." He added, as a footnote: "The wind is your own breathing, fairly heavy at the time, if I remember; your interlocked pulses produced the thunder effect."

Maxted drifted in a wash of sound.

Some while later Sheringham's face filled his eyes, beard wagging, mouth working wildly.

"Maxted! You've only two more guesses, so for God's sake concentrate," he shouted irritably, his voice almost lost among the thunder rolling from the sea. "Come on, man, what is it? Maxted!" he bellowed. He leapt for the nearest loudspeaker and drove up the volume. The sound boomed out of the patio, reverberating into the night.

Maxted had almost gone now, his fading identity a small featureless island nearly eroded by the waves beating across it.

Sheringham knelt down and shouted into his ear.

"Maxted, can you hear the sea? Do you know where you're drowning?"

A succession of gigantic flaccid waves, each more lumbering and enveloping than the last, rode down upon them.

"In a kiss!" Sheringham screamed. A kiss!"

The island slipped and slid away into the molten shelf of the sea.

THE WATCH-TOWERS

THE NEXT DAY, for some reason, there was a sudden increase of activity in the watch-towers. This began during the latter half of the morning, and by noon, when Renthall left the hotel on his way to see Mrs. Osmond, seemed to have reached its peak. People were standing at their windows and balconies along both sides of the street, whispering agitatedly to each other behind the curtains and pointing up into the sky.

Renthall usually tried to ignore the watch-towers, resenting even the smallest concession to the fact of their existence, but at the bottom of the street, where he was hidden in the shadow thrown by one of the houses, he stopped and craned his head up at the nearest tower.

A hundred feet away from him, it hung over the Public Library, its tip poised no more than twenty feet above the roof. The glass-enclosed cabin in the lowest tier appeared to be full of observers, opening and shutting the windows and shifting about what Renthall assumed were huge pieces of optical equipment. He looked around at the further towers, suspended from the sky at three hundred feet intervals in every direction, noticing an occasional flash of light as a window turned and caught the sun.

An elderly man wearing a shabby black suit and wing collar, who usually loitered outside the library, came across the street to Renthall and backed into the shadows beside him.

"They're up to something all right." He cupped his hands over his eyes and peered up anxiously at the watch-towers. "I've never seen them like this as long as I can remember."

Renthall studied his face. However alarmed, he was obviously relieved by the signs of activity. "I shouldn't worry unduly," Renthall told him. "It's a change to see something going on at all."

Before the other could reply he turned on his heel and strode away along the pavement. It took him ten minutes to reach the street in which Mrs. Osmond lived, and he fixed his eyes firmly on the ground, ignoring the few passers-by. Although dominated by the watch-towers—four of them hung in a line exactly down its centre—the street was almost deserted. Half the houses were untenanted and falling into what would soon be an irreversible state of disrepair. Usually Renthall assessed each property carefully, trying to decide whether to leave his hotel and take one of them, but the movement in the watch-towers had caused him more anxiety than he was prepared to admit, and the terrace of houses passed unnoticed.

Mrs. Osmond's house stood half-way down the street, its gate swinging loosely on its rusty hinges. Renthall hesitated under the plane tree growing by the edge of the pavement, and then crossed the narrow garden and quickly let himself through the door.

Mrs. Osmond invariably spent the afternoon sitting out on the veranda in the sun, gazing at the weeds in the back garden, but today she had retreated to a corner of the sitting room. She was sorting a suitcase full of old papers when Renthall came in.

Renthall made no attempt to embrace her and wandered over to the window. Mrs. Osmond had half drawn the curtains and he pulled them back. There was a watch-tower ninety feet away, almost directly ahead, hanging over the parallel terrace of empty houses. The lines of towers receded diagonally from left to right towards the horizon, partly obscured by the bright haze.

"Do you think you should have come today?" Mrs. Osmond asked, shifting her plump hips nervously in the chair.

"Why not?" Renthall said, scanning the towers, hands loosely in his pockets.

"But if they're going to keep a closer watch on us now they'll notice you coming here."

"I shouldn't believe all the rumours you hear," Renthall told her calmly.

"What do you think it means then?"

"I've absolutely no idea. Their movements may be as random and meaningless as our own." Renthall shrugged. "Perhaps they *are* going to keep a closer watch on us. What does it matter if all they do is stare?"

"Then you mustn't come here any more!" Mrs. Osmond protested.

"Why? I hardly believe they can see through walls."

"They're not that stupid," Mrs. Osmond said irritably. "They'll soon put two and two together, if they haven't already."

Renthall took his eyes off the tower and looked down at Mrs. Osmond patiently. "My dear, this house isn't tapped.

For all they know we may be darning our prayer rugs or discussing the endocrine system of the tapeworm."

"Not you, Charles," Mrs. Osmond said with a short laugh. "Not if they know you." Evidently pleased by this sally, she relaxed and took a cigarette out of the box on the table.

"Perhaps they don't know me," Renthall said dryly. "In fact, I'm quite sure they don't. If they did I can't believe I should still be here."

He noticed himself stooping, a reliable sign that he was worrying, and went over to the sofa.

"Is the school going to start tomorrow?" Mrs. Osmond asked when he had disposed his long thin legs around the table.

"It should do," Renthall said. "Hanson went down to the Town Hall this morning, but as usual they had little idea or what was going on."

He opened his jacket and pulled out of the inner pocket an old but neatly folded copy of a woman's magazine.

"Charles!" Mrs. Osmond exclaimed. "Where did you get this?"

She took it from Renthall and started leafing through the soiled pages.

"One of my sources," Renthall said. From the sofa he could still see the watch-tower over the houses opposite. "Georgina Simons. She has a library of them."

He rose, went over to the window and drew the curtains across.

"Charles, don't. I can't see."

"Read it later," Renthall told her. He lay back on the sofa again. "Are you coming to the recital this afternoon?"

"Hasn't it been cancelled?" Mrs. Osmond asked, putting the magazine down reluctantly.

"No, of course not."

"Charles, I don't think I want to go." Mrs. Osmond frowned. "What records is Hanson going to play?"

"Some Tchaikovsky. And Grieg." He tried to make it sound interesting. "You must come. We can't just sit about subsiding into this state of boredom and uselessness."

"I know," Mrs. Osmond said fractiously. "But I don't feel like it. Not today. All those records bore me. I've heard them so often."

"They bore me too. But at least it's something to do." He put his arm around Mrs. Osmond's shoulders and began to play with the darker unbleached hair behind her ears, tapping the large nickel earrings she wore and listening to them tinkle.

When he put his hand on to her knee Mrs. Osmond stood up and prowled aimlessly around the room, straightening her skirt.

"Julia, what is the matter with you?" Renthall asked irritably. "Have you got a headache?"

Mrs. Osmond was by the window, gazing up at the watchtowers. "Do you think they're going to come down?"

"Of course not!" Renthall snapped. "Where on earth did you get that idea?"

Suddenly he felt unbearably exasperated. The confined dimensions of the dusty sitting room seemed to suffocate reason. He stood up and buttoned his jacket. "I'll see you this afternoon at the Institute, Julia. The recital starts at three."

Mrs. Osmond nodded vaguely, unfastened the french windows and ambled forward across the veranda into full view of the watch-towers, the glassy expression on her face like a supplicant nun's.

As Renthall had expected, the school did not open the next day. When they tired of hanging around the hotel after breakfast he and Hanson went down to the Town Hall. The building was almost empty and the only official they were able to find was unhelpful.

"We have no instructions at present," he told them, "but as soon as the term starts you will be notified. Though from what I hear the postponement is to be indefinite."

"Is that the committee's decision?" Renthall asked. "Or just another of the town clerk's brilliant extemporisings?"

"The school committee is no longer meeting," the official said. "I'm afraid the town clerk isn't here today." Before Renthall could speak he added: "You will, of course, continue to draw your salaries. Perhaps you would care to call in at the treasurer's department on your way out?"

Renthall and Hanson left and looked about for a cafe. Finally they found one that was open and sat under the awning, staring vacantly at the watch-towers hanging over the roof-tops around them. Their activity had lessened considerably since the previous day. The nearest tower was only fifty feet away, immediately above a disused office building on the other side of the street. The windows in the observation tier remained shut, but every few minutes Renthall noticed a shadow moving behind the panes.

Eventually a waitress came out to them, and Renthall ordered coffee.

"I think I shall have to give a few lessons," Hanson remarked. "All this leisure is becoming too much of a good thing."

"It's an idea," Renthall agreed. "If you can find anyone interested. I'm sorry the recital yesterday was such a flop."

Hanson shrugged. "I'll see if I can get hold of some new records. By the way, I thought Julia looked very handsome yesterday."

Renthall acknowledged the compliment with a slight bow of his head. "I'd like to take her out more often."

"Do you think that's wise?"

"Why on earth not?"

"Well, just at present, you know." Hanson inclined a finger at the watch-towers.

"I don't see that it matters particularly," Renthall said. He disliked personal confidences and was about to change the subject when Hanson leaned forward across the table.

"Perhaps not, but I gather there was some mention of you at the last Council meeting. One or two members were rather critical of your little menage a deux." He smiled thinly at Renthall, who was frowning into his coffee. "Sheer spite, no doubt, but your behaviour is a little idiosyncratic."

Controlling himself, Renthall pushed away the coffee cup. "Do you mind telling me what damned business it is of theirs?"

Hanson laughed. "None, really, except that they are the executive authority, and I suppose we should take our cue from them." Renthall snorted at this, and Hanson went on: "As a matter of interest, you may receive an official directive over the next few days."

"A *what?*" Renthall exploded. He sat back, shaking his head incredulously. "Are you serious?" When Hanson nodded he began to laugh harshly. "Those idiots! I don't know why we put up with them. Sometimes their stupidity positively staggers me."

"Steady on," Hanson demurred. "I do see their point. Bearing in mind the big commotion in the watch-towers yesterday the Council probably feel we shouldn't do anything that might antagonise them. You never know, they may even be acting on official instructions."

Renthall glanced contemptuously at Hanson. "Do you *really* believe that nonsense about the Council being in touch with the watch-towers? It may give a few simpletons a sense of security, but for heaven's sake don't try it on me. My patience is just about exhausted." He watched Hanson carefully, wondering which of the Council members had provided him with his information. The lack of subtlety depressed him painfully. "However, thanks for warning me. I suppose it means there'll be an overpowering air of embarrassment when Julia and I go to the cinema tomorrow."

Hanson shook his head. "No. Actually the performance has been cancelled. In view of yesterday's disturbances."

"But why——?" Renthall slumped back. "Haven't they got the intelligence to realise that it's just at this sort of time that we need every social get-together we can organise? People are hiding away in their back bedrooms like a lot of frightened ghosts. We've got to bring them out, give them something that will pull them together."

He gazed up thoughtfully at the watch-tower across the street. Shadows circulated behind the frosted panes of the observation windows. "Some sort of gala, say, or a garden fete. Who could organise it, though?"

Hanson pushed back his chair. "Careful, Charles. I don't know whether the Council would altogether approve."

"I'm sure they wouldn't." After Hanson had left he remained at the table and returned to his solitary contemplation of the watch-towers.

For half an hour Renthall sat at the table, playing absently with his empty coffee cup and watching the few people who passed along the street. No one else visited the cafe, and he was glad to be able to pursue his thoughts alone, in this miniature urban vacuum, with nothing to intervene between himself and the lines of watch-towers stretching into the haze beyond the roof-tops.

With the exception of Mrs. Osmond, Renthall had virtually no close friends in whom to confide. With his sharp intelligence and impatience with trivialities, Renthall was one of those men with whom others find it difficult to relax. A certain innate condescension, a reserved but unmistakable attitude of superiority held them away from him, though few people regarded him as anything but a shabby pedagogue. At the hotel he kept to himself. There was little social contact between the guests; in the lounge and dining room they sat immersed in their old newspapers and magazines, occasionally murmuring quietly to each other. The only thing which could mobilise the simultaneous communion of the guests was some untoward activity in the watch-towers, and at such times Renthall always maintained an absolute silence.

Just before he stood up a square thick-set figure approached down the street. Renthall recognised the man and was about to turn his seat to avoid having to greet him, but something about his expression made him lean forward.

Fleshy and dark-jowelled, the man walked with an easy rolling gait, his double-breasted check overcoat open to reveal a well-tended midriff. This was Victor Boardman, owner of the local flea-pit cinema, sometime bootlegger and procurer at large.

Renthall had never spoken to him, but he was aware that Boardman shared with him the distinction of bearing the stigma of the Council's disapproval. Hanson claimed that the Council had successfully stamped out Boardman's illicit activities, but the latter's permanent expression of smug contempt for the rest of the world seemed to belie this.

As he passed they exchanged glances, and Boardman's face broke momentarily into a knowing smirk. It was obviously directed at Renthall, and implied a pre-judgment of some event about which Renthall as yet knew nothing, presumably his coming collision with the Council. Obviously Boardman expected him to capitulate to the Council without a murmur.

Annoyed, Renthall turned his back on Boardman, then watched him over his shoulder as he padded off down the street, his easy relaxed shoulders swaying from side to side.

The following day the activity in the watch-towers had subsided entirely. The blue haze from which they extended was brighter than it had been for several months, and the air in the streets seemed to sparkle with the light reflected off the observation windows. There was no sign of movement among them, and the sky had a rigid uniform appearance that indicated an indefinite lull.

For some reason, however, Renthall found himself more nervous than he had been for some time. The school had not yet opened, but he felt strangely reluctant to visit Mrs. Osmond and remained indoors all morning, shunning the streets as if avoiding some invisible shadow of guilt.

The long lines of watch-towers stretching endlessly from one horizon to the other reminded him that he could soon expect to receive the Council's 'directive'—Hanson would not have mentioned it by accident—and it was always during the lulls that the Council was most active in consolidating its position, issuing a stream of petty regulations and amendments.

Renthall would have liked to challenge the Council's authority on some formal matter unconnected with himself—the validity, for example, of one of the by laws prohibiting public assemblies in the street—but the prospect of all the intrigue involved in canvassing the necessary support bored him utterly. Although none of them individually would challenge the Council, most people would have been glad to see it toppled, but there seemed to be no likely focus for their opposition. Apart from the fear that the Council was in touch with the watch-towers, no one would stand up for Renthall's right to carry on his affair with Mrs. Osmond.

Curiously enough, she seemed unaware of these cross-currents when he went to see her that afternoon. She had cleaned the house and was in high humour, the windows wide open to the brilliant air.

"Charles, what's the matter with you?" she chided him when he slumped inertly into a chair. "You look like a broody hen."

"I felt rather tired this morning. It's probably the hot weather." When she sat down on the arm of the chair he put one hand listlessly on her hip, trying to summon together his energies. "Recently I've been developing an *idee fixe* about the Council, I must be going through a crisis of confidence. I need some method of re-asserting myself."

Mrs. Osmond stroked his hair soothingly with her cool fingers, her eyes watching him silkily. "What *you* need, Charles, is a little mother love. You're so isolated at that hotel, among all those old people. Why don't you rent one of the houses in this road? I'd be able to look after you then."

Renthall glanced up at her sardonically. "Perhaps I could move in here?" he asked, but she tossed her head back with a derisive snort and went over to the window.

She gazed up at the nearest watch-tower a hundred feet away, its windows closed and silent, the great shaft disappearing into the haze. "What do you suppose they're thinking about?"

Renthall snapped his fingers off-handedly. "They're probably not thinking about anything. Sometimes I wonder whether there's anyone there at all. The movements we see may be just optical illusions. Although the windows appear to open no-one's ever actually *seen* any of them. For all we know this place may well be nothing more than an abandoned zoo."

Mrs. Osmond regarded him with rueful amusement. "Charles, you do pick some extraordinary metaphors. I often doubt if you're like the rest of us, I wouldn't dare say the sort of things you do in case——" She broke off, glancing up involuntarily at the watch-towers hanging from the sky.

Idly, Renthall asked: "In case what?"

"Well, in case——" Irritably, she said: "Don't be absurd, Charles, doesn't the thought of those towers hanging down over us frighten you at all?"

Renthall turned his head slowly and stared up at the watch-towers. Once he had tried to count them, but there seemed little point. "Yes, they frightened me," he said noncommittally. "In the same way that Hanson and the old people at the hotel and everyone else here does. But not in the sense that the boys at school are frightened of *me*."

Mrs. Osmond nodded, misinterpreting this last remark. "Children are very perceptive, Charles. They probably know you're not interested in them. Unfortunately they're not old enough yet to understand what the watch-towers mean." She gave a slight shiver, and pulled her cardigan around her shoulders. "You know, on the days when they're busy behind their windows I can hardly move around, it's terrible. I feel so listless, all I want to do is sit and stare at the wall. Perhaps I'm more sensitive to their, er, radiations than most people."

Renthall smiled. "You must be. Don't let them depress you. Next time why don't you put on a paper hat and do a pirouette?"

"What? Oh, Charles, stop being cynical."

"I'm not. Seriously, Julia, do you think it would make any difference?"

Mrs. Osmond shook her head sadly. "You try, Charles, and then tell me. Where are you going?"

Renthall paused at the window. "Back to the hotel to rest. By the way, do you know Victor Boardman?"

"I used to, once. Why, what are you getting up to with him?"

"Does he own the garden next to the cinema car-park?"

"I think so." Mrs. Osmond laughed. "Are you going to take up gardening?"

"In a sense." With a wave, Renthall left.

He began with Dr. Clifton, whose room was directly below his own. Clifton's duties at his surgery occupied him for little more than an hour a day—there were virtually no deaths or illnesses—but he still retained sufficient initiative to cultivate a hobby. He had turned one end of his room into a small aviary, containing a dozen canaries, and spent much of his time trying to teach them tricks. His acerbic, matter-of-fact manner always tired Renthall, but he respected the doctor for not sliding into total lethargy like everyone else.

Clifton considered his suggestion carefully. "I agree with you, something of the sort is probably necessary. A good idea, Renthall. Properly conducted, it might well provide just the lift people need."

"The main question, doctor, is one of organisation. The only suitable place is the Town Hall."

Clifton nodded. "Yes, there's your problem. I'm afraid I've no influence with the Council, if that's what you're suggesting. I don't know what you can do. You'll have to get their permission of course, and in the past they haven't shown themselves to be very radical or original. They prefer to maintain the status quo."

Renthall nodded, then added casually: "They're only interested in maintaining their own power. At times I become rather tired of our Council."

Clifton glanced at him and then turned back to his cages. "You're preaching revolution, Renthall," he said quietly, a forefinger stroking the beak of one of the canaries. Pointedly, he refrained from seeing Renthall to the door.

Writing the doctor off, Renthall rested for a few minutes in his room, pacing up and down the strip of faded carpet, then went down to the basement to see the manager, Mulvaney.

"I'm only making some initial enquiries. As yet I haven't applied for permission, but Dr. Clifton thinks the idea is excellent, and there's no doubt we'll get it. Are you up to looking after the catering?"

Mulvaney's sallow face watched Renthall sceptically. "Of course I'm up to it, but how serious are you?" He leaned against his roll-top desk. "You think you'll get permission? You're wrong, Mr. Renthall, the Council wouldn't stand for the idea. They even closed the cinema, so they're not likely to allow a public party. Before you know what you'd have people dancing."

"I hardly think so, but does the idea appal you so much?"

Mulvaney shook his head, already bored with Renthall. "You get a permit, Mr. Renthall, and then we can talk seriously."

Tightening his voice, Renthall asked: "Is it necessary to get the Council's permission? Couldn't we go ahead without?"

Without looking up, Mulvaney sat down at his desk. "Keep trying, Mr. Renthall, it's a great idea."

During the next few days Renthall pursued his enquiries, in all approaching some half dozen people. In general he met with the same negative response, but as he intended he soon noticed a subtle but nonetheless distinct quickening of interest around him. The usual fragmentary murmur of conversation would fade away abruptly as he passed the tables in the dining room, and the service was fractionally more prompt.

Hanson no longer took coffee with him in the mornings, and once Renthall saw him in guarded conversation with the town clerk's secretary, a young man called Barnes. This, he assumed, was Hanson's contact.

In the meantime the activity in the watch-towers remained at zero. The endless lines of towers hung down from the bright hazy sky, the observation windows closed, and the people in the streets below sank slowly into their usual mindless torpor, wandering from hotel to library to cafe. Determined on his course of action, Renthall felt his confidence return.

Allowing an interval of a week to elapse, he finally called upon Victor Boardman.

The bootlegger received him in his office above the cinema, greeting him with a wry smile.

"Well, Mr. Renthall, I hear you're going into the entertainment business. Drunken gambols and all that. I'm surprised at you."

"A fete," Renthall corrected. The seat Boardman had offered him faced towards the window—deliberately, he guessed—and provided an uninterrupted view of the watchtower over the roof of the adjacent furniture store. Only forty feet away, it blocked off half the sky. The metal plates which formed its rectangular sides were annealed together by some process Renthall was unable to identify, neither welded nor riveted, almost as if the entire tower had been cast *in situ*. He moved to another chair so that his back was to the window.

"The school is still closed, so I thought I'd try to make myself useful. That's what I'm paid for. I've come to you because you've had a good deal of experience."

"Yes, I've had a lot of experience, Mr. Renthall. Very varied. As one of the Council's employees, I take it you have its permission?"

Renthall evaded this. "The Council is naturally a conservative body, Mr. Boardman. Obviously at this stage I'm acting on my own initiative. I shall consult the Council at the appropriate moment later, when I can offer them a practicable proposition."

Boardman nodded sagely. "That's sensible, Mr. Renthall. Now what exactly do you want me to do? Organise the whole thing for you?"

"No, but naturally I'd be very grateful if you would. For the present I merely want to ask permission to hold the fete on a piece of your property."

"The cinema? I'm not going to take all those seats out, if that's what you're after."

"Not the cinema. Though we could use the bar and cloak-rooms," Renthall extemporised, hoping the scheme did not sound too grandiose. "Is the old beer-garden next to the car park your property?"

For a moment Boardman was silent. He watched Renthall shrewdly, picking his nails with his cigar-cutter, a faint suggestion of admiration in his eyes. "So you want to hold the fete in the open, Mr. Renthall? Is that it?"

Renthall nodded, smiling back at Boardman. "I'm glad to see you living up to your reputation for getting quickly to the point. Are you prepared to lend the garden? Of course, you'll have a big share of the profits. In fact, if it's any inducement, you can have all the profits."

Boardman put out his cigar. "Mr. Renthall, you're obviously a man of many parts. I under-estimated you. I thought you merely had a grievance against the Council. I hope you know what you're doing."

"Mr. Boardman, will you lend the garden?" Renthall repeated.

There was an amused but thoughtful smile on Boardman's lips as he regarded the watch-tower framed by the window. "There are two watch-towers directly over the beer-garden, Mr. Renthall."

"I'm fully aware of that. It's obviously the chief attraction of the property. Now, can you give me an answer?"

The two men regarded each other silently, and then Boardman gave an almost imperceptible nod. Renthall realized that his scheme was being taken seriously by Boardman. He was obviously using Renthall for his own purposes, for once having flaunted the Council's authority he would be able to resume all his other, more profitable activities. Of course, the fete would never be held, but in answer to Boardman's questions he outlined a provisional programme. They fixed the date of the fete at a month ahead, and arranged to meet again at the beginning of the next week.

Two days later, as he expected, the first emissaries of the Council came to see him.

He was waiting at his usual table on the cafe terrace, the silent watch-towers suspended from the air around him, when he saw Hanson hurrying along the street.

"Do join me." Renthall drew a chair back. "What's the news?"

"Nothing—though you should know, Charles." He gave Renthall a dry smile, as if admonishing a favourite pupil, then gazed about the empty terrace for the waitress. "Service is appallingly bad here. Tell me, Charles, what's all this talk about you and Victor Boardman, I could hardly believe my ears."

Renthall leaned back in his chair. "I don't know, you tell me."

"We—er, I was wondering if Boardman was taking advantage of some perfectly innocent remark he might have overheard. This business of a garden party you're supposed to be organising with him—it sounds absolutely fantastic."

"Why?"

"But Charles." Hanson leaned forward to examine Renthall carefully, trying to make sense of his unruffled pose. "Surely you aren't serious?"

"But why not? If I want to, why shouldn't I organise a garden party—fete, to be more accurate?"

"It doesn't make an iota of difference," Hanson said tartly. "Apart from any other reason"—here he glanced skyward—"the fact remains that you are an employee of the Council."

Hands in his trouser pockets, Renthall tipped back his chair. "But that gives them no mandate to interfere in my private life. You seem to be forgetting, but the terms of my contract specifically exclude any such authority. I am not on the established grade, as my salary differential shows. If the Council disapprove, the only sanction they can apply is to give me the sack."

"They will, Charles, don't sound so smug."

Renthall let this pass. "Fair enough, if they can find anyone else to take on the job. Frankly I doubt it. They've managed to swallow their moral scruples in the past."

"Charles, this is different. As long as you're discreet no-one gives a hoot about your private affairs, but this garden party is a public matter, and well within the Council's province."

Renthall yawned. "I'm rather bored with the subject of the Council. Technically, the fete will be a private affair, by invitation only. They've no statutory right to be consulted at all. If a breach of the peace takes place the Chief Constable can take action. Why all the fuss, anyway? I'm merely trying to provide a little harmless festivity."

Hanson shook his head. "Charles, you're deliberately evading the point. According to Boardman this fete will take place out of doors—directly under two of the watch-towers. Have you realised what the repercussions would be?"

"Yes." Renthall formed the word carefully in his mouth. "Nothing. Absolutely nothing."

"Charles!" Hanson lowered his head at this apparent blasphemy, glanced up at the watch-towers over the street as if expecting instant retribution to descend from them. "Look, my dear fellow, take my advice. Drop the whole idea. You don't stand a chance anyway of ever holding this mad jape, so why deliberately court trouble with the Council? Who knows what their real power would be if they were provoked?"

Renthall rose from his seat. He looked up at the watch-tower hanging from the air on the other side of the road, controlling himself when a slight pang of anxiety stirred his heart. "I'll send you an invitation," he called back, then walked away to his hotel.

The next afternoon the town clerk's secretary called upon him in his room. During the interval, no doubt intended as a salutary pause for reflection, Renthall had remained at the hotel, reading quietly in his armchair. He paid one brief visit to Mrs. Osmond, but she seemed nervous and irritable, evidently aware of the imminent clash. The strain of maintaining an appearance of unconcern had begun to tire Renthall, and he avoided the open streets whenever possible. Fortunately the school had still not opened.

Barnes, the dapper dark-haired secretary, came straight to the point. Refusing Renthall's offer of an armchair, he held a sheet of pink duplicated paper in his hand, apparently a minute of the last Council meeting.

"Mr. Renthall, the Council has been informed of your intention to hold a garden fete in some three weeks' time. I have been asked by the chairman of the Watch Committee to express the committee's grave misgivings, and to request you accordingly to terminate all arrangements and cancel the fete immediately, pending an enquiry."

"I'm sorry, Barnes, but I'm afraid our preparations are too far advanced. We're about to issue invitations."

Barnes hesitated, casting his eye around Renthall's faded room and few shabby books as if hoping to find some ulterior motive for Renthall's behaviour.

"Mr. Renthall, perhaps I could explain that this request is tantamount to a direct order from the Council."

"So I'm aware." Renthall sat down on his window-sill and gazed out at the watch-towers. "Hanson and I went over all this, as you probably know. The Council have no more right to order me to cancel this fete than they have to stop me walking down the street."

Barnes smiled his thin bureaucratic smirk. "Mr. Renthall,

this is not a matter of the Council's statutory jurisdiction. This order is issued by virtue of the authority vested in it by its superiors. If you prefer, you can assume that the Council is merely passing on a direct instruction it has received." He inclined his head toward the watch-towers.

Renthall stood up. "Now we're at last getting down to business." He gathered himself together. "Perhaps you could tell the Council to convey to its superiors, as you call them, my polite but firm refusal. Do you get *my* point?"

Barnes retreated fractionally. He summed Renthall up carefully, then nodded. "I think so, Mr. Renthall. No doubt you understand what you're doing."

After he had gone Renthall drew the blinds over the window and lay down on his bed, for the next hour he made an effort to relax.

His final show-down with the Council was to take place the following day. Summoned to an emergency meeting of the Watch Committee, he accepted the invitation with alacrity, certain that with every member of the committee present the main council chamber would be used. This would give him a perfect opportunity to humiliate the Council by publicly calling their bluff.

Both Hanson and Mrs. Osmond assumed that he would capitulate without argument.

"Well, Charles, you brought it upon yourself," Hanson told him. "Still, I expect they'll be lenient with you. It's a matter of face now."

"More than that, I hope," Renthall replied. "They claim they were passing on a direct instruction from the watch-towers."

"Well, yes . . ." Hanson gestured vaguely. "Of course. Obviously the towers wouldn't intervene in such a trivial matter. They rely on the Council to keep a watching brief for them, as long as the Council's authority is respected they're prepared to remain aloof."

"It sounds an ideally simple arrangement. How do you think the communication between the Council and the watch-towers takes place?" Renthall pointed to the watch-tower across the street from the cabin. The shuttered observation tier hung emptily in the air like an out-of-season gondola. "By telephone? Or do they semaphor?"

But Hanson merely laughed and changed the subject.

Julia Osmond was equally vague, but equally convinced of the Council's infallibility.

"Of course they receive instructions from the towers, Charles. But don't worry, they obviously have a sense of proportion—they've been letting you come here all this time." She turned a monitory finger at Renthall, her broad-hipped bulk obscuring the towers from him. "That's your chief fault, Charles. You think you're more important than you are. Look at you now, sitting there all hunched up with your face like an old shoe. You think the Council and the watch-towers are going to give you some terrible punishment. But they won't, because you're not worth it."

Renthall picked uneagerly at his lunch at the hotel, conscious of the guests watching from the tables around him. Many had brought visitors with them, and he guessed that there would be a full attendance at the meeting that afternoon.

After lunch he retired to his room, made a desultory attempt to read until the meeting at half past two. Outside, the watch-towers hung in their long lines from the bright haze. There was no sign of movement in the observation windows, and Renthall studied them openly, hands in pockets, like a general surveying the dispositions of his enemy's forces. The haze was lower than usual, filling the interstices between the towers, so that in the distance, where the free space below their tips was hidden by the intervening roof-tops, the towers seemed to rise upwards into the air like rectangular chimneys over an industrial landscape, wreathed in white smoke.

The nearest tower was about seventy-five feet away, diagonally to his left, over the eastern end of the open garden shared by the other hotels in the crescent. Just as Renthall turned away, one of the windows in the observation deck appeared to open, the opaque glass pane throwing a spear of sharp sunlight directly towards him. Renthall flinched back, heart suddenly surging, then leaned forward again. The activity in the tower had subsided as instantly as it had arisen. The windows were sealed, no signs of movement behind them. Renthall listened to the sounds from the rooms above and below him. So conspicuous a motion of the window, the first sign of activity for many days, and a certain indication of more to come, should have brought a concerted rush to the balconies. But the hotel was silent, and below he could hear Dr. Clifton at his cages by the window, humming absently to himself.

Renthall scanned the windows on the other side of the garden but the lines of craning faces he expected were absent. He examined the watch-tower carefully, assuming that he had seen a window open in a hotel nearby. Yet the explanation dissatisfied him. The ray of sunlight had cleaved the air like a silver blade, with a curious luminous intensity that only the windows of the watch-towers seemed able to reflect, aimed unerringly at his head.

He broke off to glance at his watch, cursed when he saw that it was after quarter past two. The Town Hall was a good half mile away, and he would arrive dishevelled and perspiring.

There was a knock on his door. He opened it to find Mulvaney.

"What is it? I'm busy now."

"Sorry, Mr. Renthall. A man called Barnes from the Council asked me to give you an urgent message. He said the meeting this afternoon has been postponed."

"Ha!" Leaving the door open, Renthall snapped his fingers contemptuously at the air. "So they've had second thoughts after all. Discretion is the better part of valour." Smiling broadly, he called Mulvaney back into his room. "Mr. Mulvaney! Just a moment!"

"Good news, Mr. Renthall?"

"Excellent. I've got them on the run." He added: "You wait and see, the next meeting of the Watch Committee will be held in private."

"You might be right, Mr. Renthall. Some people think they have over-reached themselves a bit."

"Really? That's rather interesting. Good." Renthall noted this mentally, then gestured Mulvaney over to the window. "Tell me, Mr. Mulvaney, just now while you were coming up the stairs, did you notice any activity out there?"

He gestured briefly towards the tower, not wanting to draw attention to himself by pointing at it. Mulvaney gazed out over the garden, shaking his head slowly. "Can't say I did, not more than usual. What sort of activity?"

"You know, a window opening . . ." When Mulvaney continued to shake his head, Renthall said: "Good. Let me know if that fellow Barnes calls again."

When Mulvaney had gone he strode up and down the room, whistling a Mozart rondo.

Over the next three days, however, the mood of elation gradually faded. To Renthall's annoyance no further date was fixed for the cancelled committee meeting. He had assumed that it would be held in camera, but the members must have realised that it would make little difference. Everyone would soon know that Renthall had successfully challenged their claim to be in communication with the watch-towers.

Renthall chafed at the possibility that the meeting had been postponed indefinitely. By avoiding a direct clash with

Renthall the Council had cleverly side-stepped the danger before them.

Alternatively, Renthall speculated whether he had under-estimated them. Perhaps they realised that the real target of his defiance was not the Council, but the watch-towers. The faint possibility—however hard he tried to dismiss it as childish fantasy the fear still persisted—that there *was* some mysterious collusion between the towers and the Council now began to grow in his mind. The fete had been cleverly conceived as an innocent gesture of defiance towards the towers, and it would be difficult to find something to take its place that would not be blatantly outrageous and stain him indelibly with the sin of hubris.

Besides, as he carefully reminded himself, he was not out to launch open rebellion. Originally he had reacted from a momentary feeling of pique, exasperated by the spectacle of the boredom and lethargy around him and the sullen fear with which everyone viewed the towers. There was no ques-tion of challenging their absolute authority—at least, not at this stage. He merely wanted to define the existential margins of their world—if they *were* caught in a trap, let them at least eat the cheese. Also, he calculated that it would take an affront of truly heroic scale to provoke any reaction from the watch-towers, and that a certain freedom by default was theirs, a small but valuable credit to their account built into the system.

In practical, existential terms this might well be consider-able, so that the effective boundary between black and white, between good and evil, was drawn some distance from the theoretical boundary. This watershed was the penumbral zone where the majority of the quickening pleas-ures of life were to be found, and where Renthall was most at home. Mrs. Osmond's villa lay well within its territory, and Renthall would have liked to move himself over its margins. First, though, he would have to assess the extent of this 'blue' shift, or moral parallax, but by cancelling the committee meeting the Council had effectively forestalled him.

As he waited for Barnes to call again a growing sense of frustration came over him. The watch-towers seemed to fill the sky, and he drew the blinds irritably. On the flat roof, two floors above, a continuous light hammering sounded all day, but he shunned the streets and no longer went to the cafe for his morning coffee.

Finally he climbed the stairs to the roof, through the

doorway saw two carpenters working under Mulvaney's supervision. They were laying a rough board floor over the tarred cement. As he shielded his eyes from the bright glare a third man came up the stairs behind him, carrying two sections of wooden railing.

"Sorry about the noise, Mr. Renthall," Mulvaney apologised. "We should be finished by tomorrow."

"What's going on?" Renthall asked. "Surely you're not putting a sun garden here."

"That's the idea." Mulvaney pointed to the railings. "A few chairs and umbrellas, be pleasant for the old folk. Dr. Clifton suggested it." He peered down at Renthall, who was still hiding in the doorway. "You'll have to bring a chair up here yourself, you look as if you could use a little sunshine."

Renthall raised his eyes to the watch-tower almost directly over their heads. A pebble tossed underhand would easily have rebounded off the corrugated metal underside. The roof was completely exposed to the score of watch-towers hanging in the air around them, and he wondered whether Mulvaney was out of his mind—none of the old people would sit there for more than a second.

Mulvaney pointed to a roof-top on the other side of the garden, where similar activity was taking place. A bright yellow awning was being unfurled, and two seats were already occupied.

Renthall hesitated, lowering his voice. "But what about the watch-towers?"

"The what—?" Distracted by one of the carpenters, Mulvaney turned away for a moment, then rejoined him. "Yes, you'll be able to watch everything going on from up here, Mr. Renthall."

Puzzled, Renthall made his way back to his room. Had Mulvaney misheard his question, or was this a fatuous attempt to provoke the towers? Renthall grimly visualised his responsibility if a whole series of petty acts of defiance took place. Perhaps he had accidentally tapped all the repressed resentment that had been accumulating for years?

To Renthall's amazement, a succession of creaking ascents of the staircase the next morning announced the first party of residents to use the sun deck. Just before lunch Renthall went up to the roof, found a group of at least a dozen of the older guests sitting out below the watch-tower, placidly inhaling the cool air. None of them seemed in the least perturbed by the tower. At two or three points around the crescent sunbathers had emerged, as if answering some deep latent call.

People sat on make-shift porches or leaned from the sills, calling to each other.

Equally surprising was the failure of this upsurge of activity to be followed by any reaction from the watch-towers. Half-hidden behind his blinds, Renthall scrutinised the towers carefully, once caught what seemed to be a distant flicker of movement from an observation window half a mile away, but otherwise the towers remained silent, their long ranks receding to the horizon in all directions, motionless and enigmatic. The haze had thinned slightly, and the long shafts protruded further from the sky, their outlines darker and more vibrant.

Shortly before lunch Hanson interrupted his scrutiny. "Hello, Charles. Great news! The school opens tomorrow. Thank heaven for that, I was getting so bored I could hardly stand up straight."

Renthall nodded. "Good. What's galvanised them into life so suddenly?"

"Oh, I don't know. I suppose they had to re-open sometime. Aren't you pleased?"

"Of course. Am I still on the staff?"

"Naturally. The Council doesn't bear childish grudges. They might have sacked you a week ago, but things are different now."

"What do you mean?"

Hanson scrutinised Renthall carefully. "I mean the school's opened. What is the matter, Charles?"

Renthall went over to the window, his eyes roving along the lines of sun-bathers on the roofs. He waited a few seconds in case there was some sign of activity from the watch-towers. "When's the Watch Committee going to hear my case?"

Hanson shrugged. "They won't bother now. They know you're a tougher proposition than some of the people they've been pushing around. Forget the whole thing."

"But I don't want to forget it. I want the hearing to take place. Damn it, I deliberately invented the whole business of the fete to force them to show their hand. Now they're furiously back-peddling."

"Well, what of it? Relax, they have their difficulties too." He gave a laugh. "You never know, they'd probably be only too glad of an invitation now."

"They won't get one. You know, I almost feel they've outwitted me. When the fete doesn't take place everyone will assume I've given in to them."

"But it will take place. Haven't you seen Boardman recently? He's going great guns, obviously it'll be a tremendous show. Be careful he doesn't cut you out."

Puzzled, Renthall turned from the window. "Do you mean Boardman's going ahead with it?"

"Of course. It looks like it anyway. He's got a big marquee over the car park, dozens of stalls, bunting everywhere."

Renthall drove a fist into his palm. "The man's insane!" He turned to Hanson. "We've got to be careful, something's going on. I'm convinced the Council are just biding their time, they're deliberately letting the reins go so we'll over-reach ourselves. Have you seen all these people on the roof-tops? Sun-bathing!"

"Good idea. Isn't that what you've wanted all along?"

"Not so blatantly as this." Renthall pointed to the nearest watch-tower. The windows were sealed, but the light reflected off them was far brighter than usual. "Sooner or later there'll be a short, sharp reaction. That's what the Council are waiting for."

"It's nothing to do with the Council. If people want to sit on the roof whose business is it but their own? Are you coming to lunch?"

"In a moment." Renthall stood quietly by the window, watching Hanson closely. A possibility he had not previously envisaged crossed his mind. He searched for some method of testing it. "Has the gong gone yet? My watch has stopped."

Hanson glanced at his wrist-watch. "It's twelve-thirty." He looked out through the window towards the clock tower in the distance over the Town Hall. One of Renthall's long-standing grievances against his room was that the tip of the nearby watch-tower hung directly over the clock-face, neatly obscuring it. Hanson nodded, re-setting his watch. "Twelve-thirty one. I'll see you in a few minutes."

After Hanson had gone Renthall sat on the bed, his courage ebbing slowly, trying to rationalise this unforeseen development.

The next day he came across his second case.

Boardman surveyed the dingy room distastefully, puzzled by the spectacle of Renthall hunched up in his chair by the window.

"Mr. Renthall, there's absolutely no question of cancelling it now. The fair's as good as started already. Anyway, what would be the point?"

"Our arrangement was that it should be a fete," Renthall pointed out. "You've turned it into a fun-fair, with a lot of stalls and hurdy-gurdys."

Unruffled by Renthall's schoolmasterly manner, Boardman scoffed. "Well, what's the difference? Anyway, my real idea is to roof it over and turn it into a permanent amusement park. The Council won't interfere. They're playing it quiet now."

"Are they? I doubt it." Renthall looked down into the garden. People sat about in their shirt sleeves, the women in floral dresses, evidently oblivious of the watch-towers filling the sky a hundred feet above their heads. The haze had receded still further, and at least two hundred yards of shaft were now visible. There were no signs of activity from the towers, but Renthall was convinced that this would soon begin.

"Tell me," he asked Boardman in a clear voice. "Aren't you frightened of the watch-towers?"

Boardman seemed puzzled. "The what towers?" He made a spiral motion with his cigar. "You mean the big slide? Don't worry I'm not having one of those, nobody's got the energy to climb all those steps."

He stuck his cigar in his mouth and ambled to the door. "Well, so long, Mr. Renthall. I'll send you an invite."

Later that afternoon Renthall went to see Dr. Clifton in his room below.

"Excuse me, doctor," he apologised, "but would you mind seeing me on a professional matter?"

"Well, not here, Renthall, I'm supposed to be off-duty." He turned from his canary cages by the window with a testy frown, then relented when he saw Renthall's intent expression. "All right, what's the trouble?"

While Clifton washed his hands Renthall explained. "Tell me, doctor, is there any mechanism known to you by which the simultaneous hypnosis of large groups of people could occur? We're all familiar with theatrical displays of the hypnotist's art, but I'm thinking of a situation in which the members of an entire small community—such as the residents of the hotels around this crescent—could be induced to accept a given proposition completely conflicting with reality."

Clifton stopped washing his hands. "I thought you wanted to see me professionally. I'm a doctor, not a witch doctor. What are you planning now, Renthall? Last week it was a fete, now you want to hypnotise an entire neighbourhood, you'd better be careful."

Renthall shook his head. "It's not I who want to carry out the hypnosis, Doctor. In fact I'm afraid the operation has already taken place. I don't know whether you've noticed anything strange about your patients?"

"Nothing more than usual," Clifton remarked dryly. He watched Renthall with increased interest. "Who's responsible for this mass hypnosis?" When Renthall paused and then pointed a forefinger at the ceiling Clifton nodded sagely. "I see. How sinister."

"Exactly. I'm glad you understand, doctor." Renthall went over to the window, looking out at the sun-shades below. He pointed to the watch-towers. "Just to clarify a small point, doctor. You do see the watch-towers?"

Clifton hesitated fractionally, moving imperceptibly towards his valise on the desk. Then he nodded: "Of course."

"Good. I'm relieved to hear it." Renthall laughed. "For a while I was beginning to think that I was the only one in step. Do you realise that both Hanson and Boardman can no longer see the towers? And I'm fairly certain that none of the people down there can or they wouldn't be sitting in the open. I'm convinced that this is the Council's doing, but it seems unlikely that they would have enough power——" He broke off, aware that Clifton was watching him fixedly. "What's the matter? *Doctor!*"

Clifton quickly took his prescription pad from his valise. "Renthall, caution is the essence of all strategy. It's important that we beware of over-hastiness. I suggest that we both rest this afternoon. Now, these will give you some sleep——"

For the first time in several days he ventured out into the street. Head down, angry for being caught out by the doctor, he drove himself along the pavement towards Mrs. Osmond, determined to find at least one person who could still see the towers. The streets were more crowded than he could remember for a long time and he was forced to look upward as he swerved in and out of the ambling pedestrians. Overhead, like the assault craft from which some apocalyptic air-raid would be launched, the watch-towers hung down from the sky, framed between the twin spires of the church, blocking off a vista down the principle boulevard, yet unperceived by the afternoon strollers.

Renthall passed the cafe, surprised to see the terrace packed with coffee-drinkers, then saw Boardman's marquee in the cinema car park. Music was coming from a creaking wurlitzer, and the gay ribbons of the bunting fluttered in the air.

Twenty yards from Mrs. Osmond's he saw her come through her front door, a large straw hat on her head.

"Charles! What are you doing here? I haven't seen you for days, I wondered what was the matter."

Renthall took the key from her fingers and pushed it back

into the lock. Closing the door behind them, he paused in the darkened hall, regaining his breath.

"Charles, what on earth is going on? Is someone after you? You look terrible, my dear. Your face—"

"Never mind my face." Renthall collected himself, and led the way into the living room. "Come in here, quickly." He went over to the window and drew back the blinds, ascertained that the watch-tower over the row of houses opposite was still there. "Sit down and relax. I'm sorry to rush in like this but you'll understand in a minute." He waited until Mrs. Osmond settled herself reluctantly on the sofa, then rested his palms on the mantelpiece, organising his thoughts.

"The last few days have been fantastic, you wouldn't believe it, and to cap everything I've just made myself look the biggest possible fool in front of Clifton. God, I could—"

"Charles—!"

"*Listen!* Don't start interrupting me before I've begun, I've got enough to contend with. Something absolutely insane is going on everywhere, by some freak I seem to be the only one who's still compus mentis. I know that sounds as if I'm completely mad, but in fact it's true. Why I don't know, though I'm frightened it may be some sort of reprisal directed at me. However." He went over to the window. "Julia, what can you see out of that window?"

Mrs. Osmond dismantled her hat and squinted at the panes. She fidgeted uncomfortably. "Charles, what is going on?— I'll have to get my glasses." She subsided helplessly.

"Julia! You've never needed your glasses before to see these. Now tell me, what can you see?"

"Well, the row of houses, and the gardens . . ."

"Yes, what else?"

"The windows, of course, and there's a tree . . ."

"What about the sky?"

She nodded. "Yes, I can see that, there's a sort of haze, isn't there? Or is that my eyes?"

"No." Wearily, Renthall turned away from the window. For the first time a feeling of unassuagable fatigue had come over him. "Julia," he asked quietly. "Don't you remember the watch-towers?"

She shook her head slowly. "No, I don't. Where were they?" A look of concern came over her face. She took his arm gently. "Dear, what is going on?"

Renthall forced himself to stand upright. "I don't know." He drummed his forehead with his free hand. "You can't remember the towers at all, or the observation windows?"

He pointed to the watch-tower hanging down the centre of the window. "There—used to be one over those houses. We were always looking at it. Do you remember how we used to draw the curtains upstairs?"

"Charles! Be careful, people will hear. Where are you going?"

Numbly, Renthall pulled back the door. "Outside," he said in a flat voice. "There's little point now in staying indoors."

He let himself through the front door, fifty yards from the house heard her call after him, turned quickly into a side road and hurried towards the first intersection.

Above him he was conscious of the watch-towers hanging in the bright air, but he kept his eyes level with the gates and hedges, scanning the empty houses. Now and then he passed one that was occupied, the family sitting out on the lawn, and once someone called his name, reminding him that the school had started without him. The air was fresh and crisp, the light glimmering off the pavements with an unusual intensity.

Within ten minutes he realised that he had wandered into an unfamiliar part of the town and completely lost himself, with only the aerial lines of watch-towers to guide him, but he still refused to look up at them.

He had entered a poorer quarter of the town, where the narrow empty streets were separated by large waste dumps, and tilting wooden fences sagged between ruined houses. Many of the dwellings were only a single storey high, and the sky seemed even wider and more open, the distant watch-towers along the horizon like a continuous palisade.

He twisted his foot on a ledge of stone, and hobbled painfully towards a strip of broken fencing that straddled a small rise in the centre of the waste dump. He was perspiring heavily, and loosened his tie, then searched the surrounding straggle of houses for a way back into the streets through which he had come.

Overhead, something moved and caught his eye. Forcing himself to ignore it, Renthall regained his breath, trying to master the curious dizziness that touched his brain. An immense sudden silence hung over the waste ground, so absolute that it was as if some inaudible piercing music was being played at full volume.

To his right, at the edge of the waste ground, he heard feet shuffle slowly across the rubble, and saw the elderly man in the shabby black suit and wing collar who usually loitered outside the public library. He hobbled along, hands in pockets, an almost Chaplinesque figure, his weak eyes now and then feebly scanning the sky as if he were searching for something he had lost or forgotten.

Renthall watched him cross the waste ground, but before he could shout the decrepit figure tottered away behind a ruined wall.

Again something moved above him, followed by a third sharp angular motion, and then a succession of rapid shuttles. The stony rubbish at his feet flickered with the reflected light, and abruptly the whole sky sparkled as if the air was opening and shutting.

Then, as suddenly, everything was motionless again.

Composing himself, Renthall waited for a last moment. Then he raised his face to the nearest watch-tower fifty feet above him, and gazed across at the hundreds of towers that hung from the clear sky like giant pillars. The haze had vanished and the shafts of the towers were defined with unprecedented clarity.

As far as he could see, all the observation windows were open. Silently, without moving, the watchers stared down at him.

A QUESTION OF RE-ENTRY

ALL DAY they had moved steadily upstream, occasionally pausing to raise the propeller and cut away the knots of weed, and by 3 o'clock had covered some seventy-five miles. Fifty yards away, on either side of the patrol launch, the high walls of the jungle river rose over the water, the unbroken massif of the mato grosso which swept across the Amazonas from Campos Buros to the delta of the Orinoco. Despite their progress—they had set off from the telegraph station at Tres Buritis at 7 o'clock that morning—the river showed no inclination to narrow or alter its volume. Sombre and unchanging, the forest followed its course, the aerial canopy shutting off the sunlight and cloaking the water along the banks with a black velvet sheen. Now and then the channel would widen into a flat expanse of what appeared to be stationary water, the slow oily swells which disturbed its surface transforming it into a huge sluggish mirror of the distant, enigmatic sky, the islands of rotten balsa logs refracted by the layers of haze like the drifting archipelagoes of a dream. Then the channel would narrow again and the cooling jungle darkness enveloped the launch.

Although for the first few hours Connolly had joined Captain Pereira at the rail, he had become bored with the endless green banks of the forest sliding past them, and since noon had remained in the cabin, pretending to study the trajectory maps. The time might pass more slowly there, but at least it was cooler and less depressing. The fan hummed and pivoted, and the clicking of the cutwater and the whispering plaint of the current past the gliding hull soothed the slight headache induced by the tepid beer he and Pereira had shared after lunch.

This first encounter with the jungle had disappointed Connolly. His previous experience had been confined to the Dredging Project at Lake Maracaibo: where the only forests consisted of the abandoned oil rigs built out into the water. Their rusting hulks, and the huge draglines and pontoons of the dredging teams, were fauna of a man-made species. In the Amazonian jungle he had expected to see the full variety of nature in its richest and most colorful outpouring, but instead it was nothing more than a moribund tree-level swamp, unweeded and overgrown, the whole thing more dead than alive, an example of bad husbandry on a continental scale. The margins of the river were rarely well defined; except where enough rotting trunks had gathered to form a firm parapet, there were no formal banks, and the shallows ran off among the undergrowth for a hundred yards irrigating huge areas of vegetation that were already drowning in moisture.

Connolly had tried to convey his disenchantment to Pereira, who now sat under the awning on the deck, placidly smoking a cheroot, partly to repay the Captain for his polite contempt for Connolly and everything his mission implied. Like all the officers of the Native Protection Missions whom Connolly had met, first in Venezuela and now in Brazil, Pereira maintained a proprietary outlook towards the jungle and its mystique, which would not be breached by any number of fresh-faced investigators in their crisp drill uniforms. Captain Pereira had not been impressed by the UN flashes on Connolly's shoulders with their orbital monogram, nor by the high-level request for assistance cabled to the Mission three weeks earlier from Brasilia. To Pereira, obviously, the office suites in the white towers at the capital were as far away as New York, London or Babylon.

Superficially, the Captain had been helpful enough, supervising the crew as they stowed Connolly's monitoring equipment aboard, checking his Smith & Wesson and exchanging a pair of defective mosquito boots. As long as Connolly had wanted to, he had conversed away amiably, pointing out this and that feature of the landscape, identifying an unusual bird or lizard on an overhead bough.

But his indifference to the real object of the mission—he had given a barely perceptible nod when Connolly described it—soon became obvious. It was this neutrality which irked Connolly, implying that Pereira spent all his time ferrying UN investigators up and down the rivers after their confounded lost space capsule like so many tourists in search of some non-existent El Dorado. Above all there was the suggestion that Connolly and the hundreds of other investigators deployed around the continent were being too persistent. When all was said and done, Pereira implied, five years had elapsed since the returning lunar spacecraft, the *Goliath 7*, had plummeted into the South American land-mass, and to prolong the search indefinitely was simply bad form, even, perhaps, necrophilic. There was not the faintest chance of the pilot still being alive, so he should be decently forgotten, given a statue outside a railway station or airport car park and left to the pigeons.

Connolly would have been glad to explain the reasons for the indefinite duration of the search, the overwhelming moral reasons, apart from the political and technical ones. He would have liked to point out that the lost astronaut, Colonel Francis Spender, by accepting the immense risks of the flight to and from the Moon, was owed the absolute discharge of any assistance that could be given him. He would have liked to remind Pereira that the successful landing on the Moon, after some half-dozen fatal attempts—at least three of the luckless pilots were still orbiting the Moon in their dead ships—was the culmination of an age-old ambition with profound psychological implications for mankind, and that the failure to find the astronaut after his return might induce unassuageable feelings of guilt and inadequacy. (If the sea was an unconscious symbol of the unconscious, was space perhaps an image of total unfettered time, and the inability to penetrate it a tragic exile to one of the limbos of eternity, a symbolic death in life?)

But Captain Pereira was not interested. Calmly inhaling the scented aroma of his cheroot, he sat imperturbably at the rail, surveying the fetid swamps that moved past them.

Shortly before noon, when they had covered some 40

miles, Connolly pointed to the remains of a bamboo landing stage elevated on high poles above the bank. A threadbare rope bridge trailed off among the mangroves, and through an embrasure in the forest they could see a small clearing where a clutter of abandoned adobe huts dissolved like refuse heaps in the sunlight.

"Is this one of their camps?"

Pereira shook his head. "The Espirro tribe, closely related to the Nambikwaras. Three years ago one of them carried influenza back from the telegraph station, an epidemic broke out, turned into a form of pulmonary edema, within forty-eight hours three hundred Indians had died. The whole group disintegrated, only about fifteen of the men and their families are still alive. A great tragedy."

They moved forward to the bridge and stood beside the tall Negro helmsman as the two other members of the crew began to shackle sections of fine wire mesh into a cage over the deck. Pereira raised his binoculars and scanned the river ahead.

"Since the Espirros vacated the area the Nambas have begun to forage down this far. We won't see any of them, but it's as well to be on the safe side."

"Do you mean they're hostile?" Connolly asked.

"Not in a conscious sense. But the various groups which comprise the Nambikwaras are permanently feuding with each other, and this far from the settlement we might easily be involved in an opportunist attack. Once we get to the settlement we'll be all right—there's a sort of precarious equilibrium there. But even so, have your wits about you. As you'll see, they're as nervous as birds."

"How does Ryker manage to keep out of their way? Hasn't he been here for years?"

"About twelve." Pereira sat down on the gunwale and eased his peaked cap off his forehead. "Ryker is something of a special case. Temperamentally he's rather explosive— I meant to warn you to handle him carefully, he might easily whip up an incident—but he seems to have maneuvered himself into a position of authority with the tribe. In some ways he's become an umpire, arbitrating in their various feuds. How he does it I haven't discovered yet; it's quite uncharacteristic of the Indians to regard a white man in that way. However, he's useful to us, we might eventually set up a mission here. Though that's next to impossible—we tried it once and the Indians just moved 500 miles away."

Connolly looked back at the derelict landing stage as it disappeared around a bend, barely distinguishable from the jungle, which was as dilapidated as this sole mournful artifact.

"What on earth made Ryker come out here?" He had heard something in Brasilia of this strange figure, sometime journalist and man of action, the self-proclaimed world citizen who at the age of forty-two, after a life spent venting his spleen on civilization and its gimcrack gods, had suddenly disappeared into the Amazonas and taken up residence with one of the aboriginal tribes. Most latter-day Gauguins were absconding con-men or neurotics, but Ryker seemed to be a genuine character in his own right, the last of a race of true individualists retreating before the barbed-wire fences and regimentation of 20th century life. But his chosen paradise seemed pretty scruffy and degenerate, Connolly reflected, when one saw it at close quarters. However, as long as the man could organize the Indians into a few search parties he would serve his purpose. "I can't understand why Ryker should pick the Amazon basin. The South Pacific, yes, but from all I've heard—and you've confirmed just now—the Indians appear to be a pretty diseased and miserable lot, hardly the noble savage."

Captain Pereira shrugged, looking away across the oily water, his plump sallow face mottled by the lace-like shadow of the wire netting. He belched discreetly to himself, and then adjusted his holster belt. "I don't know the South Pacific, but I should guess it's also been over-sentimentalized. Ryker didn't come here for a scenic tour. I suppose the Indians are diseased and, yes, reasonably miserable. Within fifty years they'll probably have died out. But for the time being they do represent a certain form of untamed, natural existence, which after all made us what we are. The hazards facing them are immense, and they survive." He gave Connolly a sly smile. "But you must argue it out with Ryker."

They lapsed into silence and sat by the rail, watching the river unfurl itself. Exhausted and collapsing, the great trees crowded the banks, the dying expiring among the living, jostling each other aside as if for a last despairing assault on the patrol boat and its passengers. For the next half an hour, until they opened their lunch packs, Connolly searched the tree-tops for the giant bifurcated parachute which should have carried the capsule to earth. Virtually impermeable to the atmosphere, it would still be visible, spreadeagled like an enormous bird over the canopy of leaves. Then, after drinking a can of Pereira's beer, he excused himself and went down to the cabin.

The two steel cases containing the monitoring equipment

had been stowed under the chart table, and he pulled them out and checked that the moisture-proof seals were still intact. The chances of making visual contact with the capsule were infinitessimal, but as long as it was intact it would continue to transmit both a sonar and radio beacon, admittedly over little more than twenty miles, but sufficient to identify its whereabouts to anyone in the immediate neighborhood. However, the entire northern half of the South Americas had been covered by successive aerial sweeps, and it seemed unlikely that the beacons were still operating. The disappearance of the capsule argued that it had sustained at least minor damage, and by now the batteries would have been corroded by the humid air.

Recently certain of the UN Space Department agencies had begun to circulate the unofficial view that Colonel Spender had failed to select the correct attitude for re-entry and that the capsule had been vaporized on its final descent, but Connolly guessed that this was merely an attempt to pacify world opinion and prepare the way for the resumption of the space program. Not only the Lake Maracaibo Dredging Project, but his own presence on the patrol boat, indicated that the Department still believed Colonel Spender to be alive, or at least to have survived the landing. His final re-entry orbit should have brought him down into the landing zone 500 miles to the east of Trinidad, but the last radio contact before the ionization layers around the capsule severed transmission indicated that he had under-shot his trajectory and come down somewhere on the South American land-mass along a line linking Lake Maracaibo with Brasilia.

Footsteps sounded down the companionway, and Captain Pereira lowered himself into the cabin. He tossed his hat onto the chart table and sat with his back to the fan, letting the air glow across his fading hair, carrying across to Connolly a sweet unsavory odor of garlic and cheap pomade.

"You're a sensible man, Lieutenant. Anyone who stays up on deck is crazy. However,"—he indicated Connolly's pallid face and hands, a memento of a long winter in New York—"in a way it's a pity you couldn't have put in some sun-bathing. That metropolitan pallor will be quite a curiosity to the Indians." He smiled agreeably, showing the yellowing teeth which made his olive complexion even darker. "You may well be the first white man in the literal sense that the Indians have seen."

"What about Ryker? Isn't he white?"

"Black as a berry now. Almost indistinguishable from the Indians, apart from being 7 feet tall." He pulled over a collection of cardboard boxes at the far end of the seat and began to rummage through them. Inside was a collection of miscellaneous oddments—balls of thread and raw cotton, lumps of wax and resin, urucu paste, tobacco and seadbeads. "These ought to assure them of your good intentions."

Connolly watched as he fastened the boxes together. "How many search parties will they buy? Are you sure you brought enough? I have a fifty-dollar allocation for gifts."

"Good," Pereira said matter-of-factly. "We'll get some more beer. Don't worry, you can't buy these people, Lieutenant. You have to rely on their good-will; this rubbish will put them in the right frame of mind to talk."

Connolly smiled dourly. "I'm more keen on getting them off their hunkers and out into the bush. How are you going to organize the search parties?"

"They've already taken place."

"What?" Connolly sat forward. "How did that happen? But they should have waited"—he glanced at the heavy monitoring equipment—"they can't have known what—"

Pereira silenced him with a raised hand. "My dear Lieutenant. Relax, I was speaking figuratively. Can't you understand, these people are nomadic, they spend all their lives continually on the move. They must have covered every square foot of this forest a hundred times in the past five years. There's no need to send them out again. Your only hope is that they may have seen something and then persuade them to talk."

Connolly considered this, as Pereira unwrapped another parcel. "All right, but I may want to do a few patrols. I can't just sit around for three days."

"Naturally. Don't worry, Lieutenant. If your astronaut came down anywhere within 500 miles of here they'll know about it." He unwrapped the parcel and removed a small teak cabinet. The front panel was slotted, and lifted to reveal the face of a large ormolu table clock, its gothic hands and numerals below a gilded bell-dome. Captain Pereira compared its time with his wrist-watch. "Good. Running perfectly, it hasn't lost a second in forty-eight hours. This should put us in Ryker's good books."

Connolly shook his head. "Why on earth does he want a clock? I thought the man had turned his back on such things."

Pereira packed the tooled metal face away. "Ah, well, whenever we escape from anything we always carry a memento of it with us. Ryker collects clocks; this is the third I've bought for him. God knows what he does with them."

The launch had changed course, and was moving in a wide circle across the river, the current whispering in a tender rippling murmur across the hull. They made their way up onto the deck, where the helmsman was unshackling several sections of the wire mesh in order to give himself an uninterrupted view of the bows. The two sailors climbed through the aperture and took up their positions fore and aft, boat-hooks at the ready.

They had entered a large bow-shaped extension of the river, where the current had overflowed the bank and produced a series of low-lying mud-flats. Some two or three hundred yards wide, the water seemed to be almost motionless, seeping away through the trees which defined its margins so that the exit and inlet of the river were barely perceptible. At the inner bend of the bow, on the only firm ground, a small cantonment of huts had been built on a series of wooden palisades jutting out over the water. A narrow promontory of forest reached to either side of the cantonment, but a small area behind it had been cleared to form an open campong. On its far side were a number of wattle storage huts, a few dilapidated shacks and hovels of dried palm.

The entire area seemed deserted, but as they approached, the cutwater throwing up a fine plume of white spray across the glassy swells, a few Indians appeared in the shadows below the creepers trailing over the jetty, watching them stonily. Connolly had expected to see a group of tall broad-shouldered warriors with white markings notched across their arms and cheeks, but these Indians were puny and degenerate, their pinched faces lowered beneath their squat bony skulls. They seemed undernourished and depressed, eyeing the visitors with a sort of sullen watchfulness like pariah dogs from the gutter.

Pereira was shielding his eyes from the sun, across whose inclining path they were now moving, searching the ramshackle bungalow built of woven rattan at the far end of the jetty.

"No signs of Ryker yet. He's probably asleep or drunk." He noticed Connolly's distasteful frown. "Not much of a place, I'm afraid."

As they moved towards the jetty, the wash from the launch slapping at the greasy bamboo poles and throwing a gust of foul air into their faces, Connolly looked back across the

open disc of water, into which the curving wake of the
launch was dissolving in a final summary of their long
voyage up-river to the derelict settlement, fading into the
slack brown water like a last tenuous thread linking him
with the order and sanity of civilization. A strange atmosphere of emptiness hung over this inland lagoon, a flat pall
of dead air that in a curious way was as menacing as any
overt signs of hostility, as if the crudity and violence of all
the Amazonian jungles met here in a momentary balance
which some untoward movement of his own might upset,
unleashing appalling forces. Away in the distance, down-
shore, the great trees leaned like corpses into the glazed air,
and the haze over the water embalmed the jungle and the
late afternoon in a timeless stillness.

They bumped against the jetty, rocking lightly into the
palisade of poles and dislodging a couple of water-logged
outriggers lashed together. The helmsman reversed the engine,
waiting for the sailors to secure the lines. None of the Indians had come forward to assist them. Connolly caught a
glimpse of one old simian face regarding him with a rheumy
eye, riddled teeth nervously fingering a pouch-like lower lip.

He turned to Pereira, glad that the Captain would be in-
terceding between himself and the Indians. "Captain, I should
have asked before, but—are these Indians cannibalistic?"

Pereira shook his head, steadying himself against a
staunchion. "Not at all. Don't worry about that, they'd have
been extinct years ago if they were."

"Not even—white men?" For some reason Connolly found
himself placing a peculiarly indelicate emphasis upon the
word 'white'.

Pereira laughed, straightening his uniform jacket. "For
God's sake, Lieutenant, no. Are you worrying that your
astronaut might have been eaten by them?"

"I suppose it's a possibility."

"I assure you, there have been no recorded cases. As a
matter of interest, it's a rare practice on this continent.
Much more typical of Africa—and Europe," he added with
sly humor. Pausing to smile at Connolly, he said quietly.
"Don't despise the Indians, Lieutenant. However diseased
and dirty they may be, at least they are in equilibrium with
their environment. And with themselves. You'll find no
Christopher Columbuses or Colonel Spenders here, but no
Belsens either. Perhaps one is as much a symptom of unease
as the other?"

They had begun to drift down the jetty, over-running one
of the outriggers, whose bow creaked and disappeared under

the stern of the launch, and Pereira shouted at the helmsman: "Ahead, Sancho! More ahead! Damn Ryker, where is the man?"

Churning out a niagara of boiling brown water, the launch moved forward, driving its shoulder into the bamboo supports, and the entire jetty sprung lightly under the impact. As the motor was cut and the lines finally secured, Connolly looked up at the jetty above his head.

Scowling down at him, an expression of bilious irritability on his heavy-jawed face, was a tall bare-chested man wearing a pair of frayed cotton shorts and a sleeveless waistcoat of pleated raffia, his dark eyes almost hidden by a wide-brimmed straw hat. The heavy muscles of his exposed chest and arms were the color of tropical teak, and the white scars on his lips and the fading traces of the heat ulcers which studded his shin bones provided the only lighter coloring. Standing there, arms akimbo with a sort of jaunty arrogance, he seemed to represent to Connolly that quality of untamed energy which he had so far found so conspicuously missing from the forest.

Completing his scrutiny of Connolly, the big man bellowed: "Pereira, for God's sake, what do you think you're doing? That's my bloody outrigger you've just run down! Tell that steersman of yours to get the cataracts out of his eyes or I'll put a bullet through his backside!"

Grinning good humoredly, Pereira pulled himself up on to the jetty. "My dear Ryker, contain yourself. Remember your blood-pressure." He peered down at the water-logged hulk of the derelict canoe which was now ejecting itself slowly from the river. "Anyway, what good is a canoe to you, you're not going anywhere."

Grudgingly, Ryker shook Pereira's hand. "That's what you like to think, Captain. You and your confounded Mission, you want me to do all the work. Next time you may find I've gone a thousand miles up-river. And taken the Nambas with me."

"What an epic prospect, Ryker. You'll need a Homer to celebrate it." Pereira turned and gestured Connolly on to the jetty. The Indians were still hanging about listlessly, like guilty intruders.

Ryker eyed Connolly's uniform suspiciously. "Who's this? Another so-called anthropologist, sniffing about for smut? I warned you last time, I will not have any more of those."

"No, Ryker. Can't you recognize the uniform? Let me introduce Lieutenant Connolly, of that brotherhood of latter-day saints, by whose courtesy and generosity we live in peace together—the United Nations."

"What? Don't tell me they've got a mandate here now? God above, I suppose he'll bore my head off about cereal/ protein rations!" His ironic groan revealed a concealed reserve of acid humor.

"Relax. The Lieutenant is very charming and polite. He works for the Space Department, Reclamation Division. You know, searching for lost aircraft and the like. There's a chance you may be able to help him." Pereira winked at Connolly and steered him forward. "Lieutenant, the Rajah Ryker."

"I doubt it," Ryker said dourly. They shook hands, the corded muscles of Ryker's fingers like a trap. Despite his thick-necked stoop, Ryker was a good six to ten inches taller than Connolly. For a moment he held on to Connolly's hand, a slight trace of wariness revealed below his mask of bad temper. "When did this plane come down?" he asked. Connolly guessed that he was already thinking of a profitable salvage operation.

"Some time ago," Pereira said mildly. He picked up the parcel containing the cabinet clock and began to stroll after Ryker towards the bungalow at the end of the jetty. A loweaved dwelling of woven rattan, its single room was surrounded on all sides by a veranda, the overhanging roof shading it from the sunlight. Creepers trailed across from the surrounding foliage, involving it in the background of palms and fronds, so that the house seemed a momentary formalization of the jungle.

"But the Indians might have heard something about it," Pereira went on. "Five years ago, as a matter of fact."

Ryker snorted. "My God, you've got a hope." They went up the steps on to the veranda, where a slim-shouldered Indian youth, his eyes like moist marbles, was watching from the shadows. With a snap of irritation, Ryker cupped his hand around the youth's pate and propelled him with a backward swing down the steps. Sprawling on his knees, the youth picked himself up, eyes still fixed on Connolly, then emitted what sounded like a high-pitched nasal hoot, compounded partly of fear and partly of excitement. Connolly looked back from the doorway, and noticed that several other Indians had stepped onto the pier and were watching him with the same expression of rapt curiosity.

Pereira patted Connolly's shoulder. "I told you they'd be impressed. Did you see that, Ryker?"

Ryker nodded curtly, as they entered his living room

pulled off his straw hat and tossed it on to a couch under the window. The room was dingy and cheerless. Crude bamboo shelves were strung around the walls, ornamented with a few primitive carvings of ivory and bamboo. A couple of rocking chairs and a card-table were in the center of the room, dwarfed by an immense victorian mahogany dresser standing against the rear wall. With its castellated mirrors and ornamental pediments it looked like an altar-piece stolen from a cathedral. At first glance it appeared to be leaning to one side, but then Connolly saw that its rear legs had been carefully raised from the tilting floor with a number of small wedges. In the center of the dresser, its multiple reflections receding to infinity in a pair of small wing mirrors, was a cheap three-dollar alarm clock, ticking away loudly. An over-and-under Winchester shotgun leaned against the wall beside it.

Gesturing Pereira and Connolly into the chairs, Ryker raised the blind over the rear window. Outside was the compound, the circle of huts around its perimeter. A few Indians squatted in the shadows, spears upright between their knees.

Connolly watched Ryker moving about in front of him, aware that the man's earlier impatience had given away to a faint but noticeable edginess. Ryker glanced irritably through the window, apparently annoyed to see the gradual gathering of the Indians before their huts.

There was a sweetly unsavory smell in the room, and over his shoulder Connolly saw that the card-table was loaded with a large bale of miniature animal skins, those of a vole or some other forest rodent. A half-hearted attempt had been made to trim the skins, and tags of clotted blood clung to their margins.

Ryker jerked the table with his foot. "Well, here you are," he said to Pereira. "Twelve dozen. They took a hell of a lot of getting, I can tell you. You've brought the clock?"

Pereira nodded, still holding the parcel in his lap. He gazed distastefully at the dank scruffy skins. "Have you got some rats in there, Ryker? These don't look much good. Perhaps we should check through them outside. . . ."

"Dammit, Pereira, don't be a fool!" Ryker snapped. "They're as good as you'll get. I had to trim half the skins myself. Let's have a look at the clock."

"Wait a minute." The Captain's jovial, easy-going manner had stiffened. Making the most of his temporary advantage, he reached out and touched one of the skins gingerly, shaking his head. "Pugh. . . . Do you know how much

I paid for this clock, Ryker? Seventy-five dollars. That's your credit for three years. I'm not so sure. And you're not very helpful, you know. Now about this aircraft that may have come down—"

Ryker snapped his fingers. "Forget it. Nothing did. The Nambas tell me everything." He turned to Connolly. "You can take it from me there's no trace of an aircraft around here. Any rescue mission would be wasting their time."

Pereira watched Ryker critically. "As a matter of fact it wasn't an aircraft." He tapped Connolly's shoulder flash. "It was a rocket capsule—with a man on board. A very important and valuable man. None other than the Moon pilot, Colonel Francis Spender."

"Well. . . ." Eyebrows raised in mock surprise, Ryker ambled to the window, stared out at a group of Indians who had advanced half-way across the compound. "My God, what next! The Moon pilot. Do they really think he's around here? But what a place to roost." He leaned out of the window and bellowed at the Indians, who retreated a few paces and then held their ground. "Damn fools," he muttered, "this isn't a zoo."

Pereira handed him the parcel, watching the Indians. There were more than fifty around the compound now, squatting in their doorways, a few of the younger men honing their spears. "They are remarkably curious," he said to Ryker, who had taken the parcel over to the dresser and was unwrapping it carefully. "Surely they've seen a pale-skinned man before?"

"They've nothing better to do." Ryker lifted the clock out of the cabinet with his big hands, with great care placed it beside the alarm clock, the almost inaudible motion of its pendulum lost in the metallic chatter of the latter's escapement. For a moment he gazed at the ornamental hands and numerals. Then he picked up the alarm clock and with an almost valedictory pat, like an officer dismissing a faithful if stupid minion, locked it away in the cupboard below. His former buoyancy returning, he gave Pereira a playful slap on the shoulder. "Captain, if you want any more rat-skins just give me a shout!"

Backing away, Pereira's heel touched one of Connolly's feet, distracting him from a problem he had been puzzling over since their entry into the hut. Like a concealed clue in a detective story, he was sure that he had noticed something of significance, but was unable to identify it.

"We won't worry about the skins," Pereira said. "What we'll do with your assistance, Ryker, is to hold a little parley with the chiefs, see whether they remember anything of this capsule."

Ryker stared out at the Indians now standing directly below the veranda. Irritably he slammed down the blind. "For God's sake, Pereira, they don't. Tell the Lieutenant he isn't interviewing people on Park Avenue or Piccadilly. If the Indians had seen anything I'd know."

"Perhaps." Pereira shrugged. "Still, I'm under instructions to assist Lieutenant Connolly and it won't do any harm to ask."

Connolly sat up. "Having come this far, Captain, I feel I should do two or three forays into the bush." To Ryker he explained: "They've recalculated the flight path of the final trajectory, there's a chance he may have come down further along the landing zone. Here, very possibly."

Shaking his head, Ryker slumped down on to the couch, and drove one fist angrily into the other. "I suppose this means they'll be landing here at any time with thousands of bulldozers and flame-throwers. Dammit, Lieutenant, if you have to send a man to the Moon, why don't you do it in your own back yard?"

Pereira stood up. "We'll be gone in a couple of days, Ryker." He nodded judiciously at Connolly and moved toward the door.

As Connolly climbed to his feet Ryker called out suddenly: "Lieutenant. You can tell me something I've wondered." There was an unpleasant downward curve to his mouth, and his tone was belligerent and provocative. "Why did they really send a man to the Moon?"

Connolly paused. He had remained silent during the conversation, not wanting to antagonize Ryker. The rudeness and complete self-immersion were pathetic rather than annoying. "Do you mean the military and political reasons?"

"No, I don't." Ryker stood up, arms akimbo again, measuring Connolly. "I mean the *real* reasons, Lieutenant."

Connolly gestured vaguely. For some reason formulating a satisfactory answer seemed more difficult than he had expected. "Well, I suppose you could say it was the natural spirit of exploration."

Ryker snorted derisively. "Do you seriously believe that, Lieutenant? 'The spirit of exploration!' My God! What a fantastic idea. Pereira doesn't believe that, do you Captain?"

Before Connolly could reply Pereira took his arm. "Come on, Lieutenant. This is no time for a metaphysical discussion." To Ryker he added: "It doesn't much matter what you and I believe, Ryker. A man went to the Moon and came back. He needs our help."

Ryker frowned ruefully. "Poor chap. He must be feeling pretty hungry by now. Though anyone who gets as far as the Moon and is fool enough to come back deserves what he gets."

There was a scuffle of feet on the veranda, and as they stepped out into the sunlight a couple of Indians darted away along the jetty, watching Connolly with undiminished interest.

Ryker remained in the doorway, staring listlessly at the clock, but as they were about to climb into the launch he came after them. Now and then glancing over his shoulder at the encroaching semi-circle of Indians, he gazed down at Connolly with sardonic contempt. "Lieutenant," he called out before they went below. "Has it occurred to you that if he had landed, Spender might have wanted to stay on here?"

"I doubt it, Ryker," Connolly said calmly. "Anyway, there's little chance that Colonel Spender is still alive. What we're interested in finding is the capsule."

Ryker was about to reply when a faint metallic buzz sounded from the direction of his hut. He looked around sharply, waiting for it to end, and for a moment the whole tableau, composed of the men on the launch, the gaunt outcast on the edge of the jetty and the Indians behind him, was frozen in an absurdly motionless posture. The mechanism of the old alarm clock had obviously been fully wound, and the buzz sounded for thirty seconds, finally ending with a high-pitched ping.

Pereira grinned. He glanced at his watch. "It keeps good time, Ryker." But Ryker had stalked off back to the hut, scattering the Indians before him.

Connolly watched the group dissolve, then suddenly snapped his fingers. "You're right, Captain. It certainly does keep good time," he repeated as they entered the cabin.

Evidently tired by the encounter with Ryker, Pereira slumped down among Connolly's equipment and unbuttoned his tunic. "Sorry about Ryker, but I warned you. Frankly, Lieutenant, we might as well leave now. There's nothing here. Ryker knows that. However, he's no fool, and he's quite capable of faking all sorts of evidence just to get a retainer out of you. He wouldn't mind if the bulldozers came."

"I'm not so sure." Connolly glanced briefly through the porthole. "Captain, has Ryker got a radio?"

"Of course not. Why?"

"Are you certain?"

"Absolutely. It's the last thing the man would have. Anyway, there's no electrical supply here, and he has no batteries." He noticed Connolly's intent expression. "What's on your mind, Lieutenant?"

"You're his only contact? There are no other traders in the area?"

"None. The Indians are too dangerous, and there's nothing to trade. Why do you think Ryker has a radio?"

"He must have. Or something very similar. Captain, just now you remarked on the fact that his old alarm clock kept good time. Does it occur to you to ask *how?*"

Pereira sat up slowly. "Lieutenant, you have a valid point."

"Exactly. I knew there was something odd about those two clocks when they were standing side by side. That type of alarm clock is the cheapest obtainable, notoriously inaccurate. Often they lose two or three minutes in 24 hours. But that clock was telling the right time to within ten seconds. No optical instrument would give him that degree of accuracy."

Pereira shrugged skeptically. "But I haven't been here for over four months. And even then he didn't check the time with me."

"Of course not. He didn't need to. The only possible explanation for such a degree of accuracy is that he's getting a daily time fix, either on a radio or some long-range beacon."

"Wait a moment, Lieutenant." Pereira watched the dusk light fall across the jungle. "It's a remarkable coincidence, but there must be an innocent explanation. Don't jump straight to the conclusion that Ryker has some instrument taken from the missing Moon capsule. Other aircraft have crashed in the forest. And what would be the point? He's not running an airline or railway system. Why should he need to know the time, the *exact* time, to within ten seconds?"

Connolly tapped the lid of his monitoring case, controlling his growing exasperation at Pereira's reluctance to treat the matter seriously, at his whole permissive attitude of lazy tolerance towards Ryker, the Indians and the forest. Obviously he unconsciously resented Connolly's sharp-eyed penetration of this private world.

"Clocks have become his idée fixe," Pereira continued. "Perhaps he's developed an amazing sensitivity to its mechanism. Knowing exactly the right time could be a substitute for the civilization on which he turned his back." Thoughtfully, Pereira moistened the end of his cheroot. "But I agree that it's strange. Perhaps a little investigation would be worth while after all."

After a cool jungle night in the air-conditioned cabin, the next day Connolly began discreetly to reconnoitre the area. Pereira took ashore two bottles of whiskey and a soda syphon, and was able to keep Ryker distracted while Connolly roved about the campong with his monitoring equipment. Once or twice he heard Ryker bellow jocularly at him from his window as he lolled back over the whiskey. At intervals, as Ryker slept, Pereira would come out into the sun, sweating like a drowsy pig in his stained uniform, and try to drive back the Indians.

"As long as you stay within earshot of Ryker you're safe," he told Connolly. Chopped-out pathways criss-crossed the bush at all angles, a fresh pathway driven through the foliage whenever one of the bands returned to the campong, irrespective of those already established. This maze extended for miles around them. "If you get lost, don't panic but stay where you are. Sooner or later we'll come out and find you."

Eventually giving up his attempt to monitor any of the signal beacons built into the lost capsule—both the sonar and radio meters remained at zero—Connolly tried to communicate with the Indians by sign language, but with the exception of one, the youth with the moist limpid eyes who had been hanging about on Ryker's veranda, they merely stared at him stonily. This youth Pereira identified as the son of the former witch-doctor ("Ryker's more or less usurped his role, for some reason the old boy lost the confidence of the tribe"). While the other Indians gazed at Connolly as if seeing some invisible numinous shadow, some extra-corporeal nimbus which pervaded his body, the youth was obviously aware that Connolly possessed some special talent, perhaps not dissimilar from that which his father had once practised. However, Connolly's attempts to talk to the youth were handicapped by the fact that he was suffering from a purulent ophthalmia, gonococchic in origin and extremely contagious, which made his eyes water continuously. Many of the Indians suffered from this complaint, threatened by permanent blindness, and Connolly had seen them treating their eyes with water in which a certain type of fragrant bark had been dissolved.

Ryker's casual, off-hand authority over the Indians puzzled Connolly. Slumped back in his chair against the mahogany dresser, one hand touching the ormolu clock, most of the time he and Pereira indulged in a lachrymose back-chat. Then, oblivious of any danger, Ryker would amble out into the dusty campong, push his way blurrily through the Indians and drum up a party to collect fire wood for the water still, jerking them bodily to their feet as they squatted about their huts. What interested Connolly was the Indians' reaction to this type of treatment. They seemed to be restrained, not by any belief in his strength of personality or primitive kingship, but by a grudging acceptance that for the time being at any rate, Ryker possessed the whip hand over them all. Obviously Ryker served certain useful roles for them as an intermediary with the Mission, but this alone would not explain the sources of his power. Beyond certain more or less defined limits—the perimeter of the campong —his authority was minimal.

A hint of explanation came on the second morning of their visit, when Connolly accidentally lost himself in the forest.

*   *   *

After breakfast Connolly sat under the awning on the deck of the patrol launch, gazing out over the brown, jelly-like surface of the river. The campong was silent. During the night the Indians had disappeared into the bush. Like lemmings they were apparently prone to these sudden irresistible urges. Occasionally the nomadic call would be strong enough to carry them 200 miles away; at other times they would set off in high spirits and then lose interest after a few miles, returning dispiritedly to the campong in small groups.

Deciding to make the most of their absence, Connolly shouldered the monitoring equipment and climbed onto the pier. A few dying fires smoked plaintively among the huts, and abandoned utensils and smashed pottery lay about in the red dust. In the distance the morning haze over the forest had lifted, and Connolly could see what appeared to be a low hill—a shallow rise no more than a hundred feet in height—which rose off the flat floor of the jungle a quarter of a mile away.

On his right, among the huts, someone moved. An old man sat alone among the refuse of pottery shards and raffia baskets, cross-legged under a small make-shift awning. Barely distinguishable from the dust, his diseased moribund figure seemed to contain the whole futility and degradation of the Amazon forest.

Still musing on Ryker's motives for isolating himself in the jungle, Connolly made his way towards the distant rise.

Ryker's behavior the previous evening had been curious. Shortly after dusk, when the sunset sank into the western forest, bathing the jungle in an immense ultramarine and golden light, the day-long chatter and movement of the Indians ceased abruptly. Connolly had been glad of the silence—the endless thwacks of the rattan canes and grating of the stone mills in which they mixed the Government-issue meal had become tiresome. Pereira made several cautious visits to the edge of the campong, and each time reported that the Indians were sitting in a huge circle outside their huts, watching Ryker's bungalow. The latter was lounging on his veranda in the moonlight, chin in hand, one boot up on the rail, morosely surveying the assembled tribe.

"They've got their spears and ceremonial feathers," Pereira whispered. "For a moment I almost believed they were preparing an attack."

After waiting half an hour, Connolly climbed up on to the pier, found the Indians squatting in their dark silent circle, Ryker glaring down at them. Only the witch-doctor's son made any attempt to approach Connolly, sidling tentatively through the shadows, a piece of what appeared to be blue obsidian in his hand, some talisman of his father's that had lost its potency.

Uneasily, Connolly returned to the launch, and shortly after 3 a.m. they were wakened in their bunks by a tremendous whoop, reached the deck to hear the stampede of feet through the dust, the hissing of overturned fires and cooking pots. Apparently leading the pack, Ryker, emitting a series of re-echoed 'Harooh's!', disappeared into the bush. Within a minute the campong was empty.

"What game is Ryker playing?" Pereira muttered as they stood on the creaking jetty in the dusty moonlight. "This must be the focus of his authority over the Nambas." Baffled, they went back to their bunks.

Reaching the margins of the rise, Connolly strolled through a small orchard which had returned to nature, hearing in his mind the exultant roar of Ryker's voice as it had cleaved the midnight jungle. Idly he picked a few of the barely ripe guavas and vividly colored cajus with their astringent delicately flavored juice. After spitting away the pith, he searched for a way out of the orchard, within a few minutes realized that he was lost.

A continuous mound when seen from the distance, the

rise was in fact a nexus of small hillocks that formed the residue of a one-time system of ox-bow lakes, and the basins between the slopes were still treacherous with deep mire. Connolly rested his equipment at the foot of a tree. Withdrawing his pistol, he fired two shots into the air in the hope of attracting Ryker and Pereira. He sat down to await his rescue, taking the opportunity to unlatch his monitors and wipe the dials.

After ten minutes no one had appeared. Feeling slightly demoralized, and frightened that the Indians might return and find him, Connolly shouldered his equipment and set off towards the north-west, in the approximate direction of the campong. The ground rose before him. Suddenly, as he turned behind a palisade of wild magnolia trees, he stepped into an open clearing on the crest of the hill.

Squatting on their heels against the tree-trunks and among the tall grass were what seemed to be the entire tribe of the Nambikwaras. They were facing him, their expressions immobile and watchful, eyes like white beads among the sheaves. Presumably they had been sitting in the clearing, only fifty yards away, when he fired his shots, and Connolly had the uncanny feeling that they had been waiting for him to make his entrance exactly at the point he had chosen.

Hesitating, Connolly tightened his grip on the radio monitor. The Indians' faces were like burnished teak, their shoulders painted with a delicate mosaic of earth colors. Noticing the spears held among the grass, Connolly started to walk on across the clearing towards a breach in the palisade of trees.

For a dozen steps the Indians remained motionless. Then, with a chorus of yells, they leapt forward from the grass and surrounded Connolly in a jabbering pack. None of them were more than five feet tall, but their plump agile bodies buffeted him about, almost knocking him off his feet. Eventually the tumult steadied itself, and two or three of the leaders stepped from the cordon and began to scrutinize Connolly more closely, pinching and fingering him with curious positional movements of the thumb and forefinger, like connoisseurs examining some interesting taxidermic object.

Finally, with a series of high-pitched whines and grunts, the Indians moved off towards the center of the clearing, propelling Connolly in front of them with sharp slaps on his legs and shoulders, like drovers goading on a large pig. They were all jabbering furiously to each other, some hacking at the grass with their machetes, gathering bundles of leaves in their arms.

Tripping over something in the grass, Connolly stumbled onto his knees. The catch slipped from the lid of the monitor, and as he stood up, fumbling with the heavy cabinet, the revolver slipped from his holster and was lost under his feet in the rush.

Giving way to his panic, he began to shout over the bobbing heads around him, to his surprise he heard one of the Indians beside him bellow to the others. Instantly, as the refrain was taken up, the crowd stopped and re-formed its cordon around him. Gasping, Connolly steadied himself, and started to search the trampled grass for his revolver, when he realized that the Indians were now staring, not at himself, but at the exposed counters of the monitor. The six meters were swinging wildly after the stampede across the clearing, and the Indians craned forward, their machetes and spears lowered, gaping at the bobbing needles.

Then there was a roar from the edge of the clearing, and a huge wild-faced man in a straw hat, a shot-gun held like a crowbar in his massive hands, stormed in among the Indians, driving them back. Dragging the monitor from his neck, Connolly felt the steadying hand of Captain Pereira take his elbow.

"Lieutenant, Lieutenant," Pereira murmured reprovingly as they recovered the pistol and made their way back to the campong, the uproar behind them fading among the undergrowth, "we were nearly in time to say grace."

*   *   *

Later that afternoon Connolly sat back in a canvas chair on the deck of the launch. About half the Indians had returned, and were wandering about the huts in a desultory manner, kicking at the fires. Ryker, his authority re-asserted, had returned to his bungalow.

"I thought you said they weren't cannibal," Connolly reminded Pereira.

The Captain snapped his fingers, as if thinking about something more important. "No they're not. Stop worrying, Lieutenant, you're not going to end up in a pot." When Connolly demurred he swung crisply on his heel. He had sharpened up his uniform, and wore his pistol belt and Sam Browne at their regulation position, his peaked cap jutting low over his eyes. Evidently Connolly's close escape had confirmed some private suspicion. "Look, they're not cannibal in the dietary sense of the term, as used by the

Good & Agriculture Organization in its classification of aboriginal peoples. They won't stalk and hunt human game in preference for any other. But—" here the Captain stared fixedly at Connolly "—in certain circumstances, after a fertility ceremonial, for example, they will eat human flesh. Like all members of primitive communities which are small numerically, the Nambikwara never bury their dead. Instead, they eat them, as a means of conserving the loss and to perpetuate the corporeal identity of the departed. Now do you understand?"

Connolly grimaced. "I'm glad to know now that I was about to be perpetuated."

Pereira looked out at the campong. "Actually they would never eat a white man, to avoid defiling the tribe." He paused. "At least, so I've always believed. It's strange, something seems to have. . . . Listen, Lieutenant," he explained, "I can't quite piece it together, but I'm convinced we should stay here for a few days longer. Various elements make me suspicious, I'm sure Ryker is hiding something. That mound where you were lost is a sort of sacred tumulus, the way the Indians were looking at your instrument made me certain that they'd seen something like it before—perhaps a panel with many flickering dials. . . . ?"

"The *Goliath 7?*" Connolly shook his head skeptically. He listened to the massive undertow of the river drumming dimly against the keel of the launch. "I doubt it, Captain. I'd like to believe you, but for some reason it just doesn't seem very likely."

"I agree. Some other explanation is preferable. But what? The Indians were squatting on that hill, waiting for someone to arrive. What else could your monitor have reminded them of?"

"Ryker's clock?" Connolly suggested. "They may regard it as a sort of ju-ju object, like a magical toy."

"No," Pereira said categorically. "These Indians are highly pragmatic, they're not impressed by useless toys. For them to be deterred from killing you means that the equipment you carried possessed some very real, down-to-earth power. Look, suppose the capsule did land here and was secretly buried by Ryker, and that in some way the clocks help him to identify its whereabouts—" here Pereira shrugged hopefully "—it's just possible."

"Hardly," Connolly said. "Besides, Ryker couldn't have buried the capsule himself, and if Colonel Spender had lived through re-entry Ryker would have helped him."

"I'm not so sure," Pereira said pensively. "It would probably strike our friend Mr. Ryker as very funny for a man to travel all the way to the Moon and back just to be killed by savages. Much too good a joke to pass over."

"What religious beliefs do the Indians have?" Connolly asked.

"No religion in the formalized sense of a creed and dogma. They eat their dead so they don't need to invent an after-life in an attempt to re-animate them. In general they subscribe to one of the so-called cargo cults. As I said, they're very material. That's why they're so lazy. Some time in the future they expect a magic galleon or giant bird to arrive carrying an everlasting cornucopia of worldly goods, so they just sit about waiting for the great day. Ryker encourages them in this idea. It's very dangerous —in some Melanesian islands the tribes with cargo cults have degenerated completely. They lie around all day on the beaches, waiting for the W.H.O. flying boat, or . . ." His voice trailed off.

Connolly nodded and supplied the unspoken thought. "Or —a space capsule?"

*   *   *

Despite Pereira's growing if muddled conviction that something associated with the missing space-craft was to be found in the area, Connolly was still skeptical. His close escape had left him feeling curiously calm and emotionless, and he looked back on his possible death with fatalistic detachment, identifying it with the total ebb and flow of life in the Amazon forests, with its myriad unremembered deaths, and with the endless vistas of dead trees leaning across the jungle paths radiating from the campong. After only two days the jungle had begun to invest his mind with its own logic, and the possibility of the space-craft landing there seemed more and more remote. The two elements belonged to different systems of natural order, and he found it increasingly difficult to visualize them overlapping. In addition there was a deeper reason for his skepticism, underlined by Ryker's reference to the 'real' reasons for the space-flights. The implication was that the entire space program was a symptom of some inner unconscious malaise afflicting mankind, and in particular the western technocracies, and that the space craft and satellites had been launched because their flights satisfied certain buried compulsions and desires. By contrast, in the jungle, where the unconscious was manifest and exposed, there was no need for these insane projections, and the likelihood of the Amazonas playing any part in the success or failure of the space flight became, by a sort of psychological parallax, increasingly blurred and distant, the missing capsule itself a fragment of a huge disintegrating fantasy.

However he agreed to Pereira's request to borrow the monitors and follow Ryker and the Indians on their midnight romp through the forest.

Once again, after dusk, the same ritual silence descended over the campong, and the Indians took up their positions in the doors of their huts. Like some morose exiled princeling, Ryker sat sprawled on his veranda, one eye on the clock through the window behind him. In the moonlight the scores of moist dark eyes never wavered as they watched him.

At last, half an hour later, Ryker galvanized his great body into life, with a series of tremendous whoops raced off across the campong, leading the stampede into the bush. Away in the distance, faintly outlined by the quarter moon, the shallow hump of the tribal tumulus rose over the black canopy of the jungle. Pereira waited until the last heel beats had subsided, then climbed onto the pier and disappeared among the shadows.

Far away Connolly could hear the faint cries of Ryker's pack as they made off through the bush, the sounds of machetes slashing at the undergrowth. An ember on the opposite side of the campong flared in the low wind, illuminating the abandoned old man, presumably the former witch doctor, whom he had seen that morning. Beside him was another slimmer figure, the limpid-eyed youth who had followed Connolly about.

A door stirred on Ryker's veranda, providing Connolly with a distant image of the white moon-lit back of the river reflected in the mirrors of the mahogany dresser. Connolly watched the door jump lightly against the latch, then walked quietly across the pier to the wooden steps.

A few empty tobacco tins lay about on the shelves around the room, and a stack of empty bottles cluttered one corner behind the door. The ormolu clock had been locked away in the mahogany dresser. After testing the doors, which had been secured with a stout padlock, Connolly noticed a dog-eared paper-backed book lying on the dresser beside a half-empty carton of cartridges.

On a faded red ground, the small black lettering on the cover was barely decipherable, blurred by the sweat from Ryker's fingers. At first glance it appeared to be a set of logarithm tables. Each of the eighty or so pages was covered with column after column of finely printed numerals and tabular material.

Curious, Connolly carried the manual over to the doorway. The title page was more explicit.

ECHO III
CONSOLIDATED TABLES OF
CELESTIAL TRAVERSES
1965-1980. TIMES
THROUGHOUT G.M.T.

Published by the National Astronautics and Space Administration, Washington, D.C., 1965. Part XV. Longitude 40-80 West, Latitude 10 North-35 South (South American Sub-Continent) Price 35¢.

His interest quickening, Connolly turned the pages. The manual fell open at the section headed: Lat. 5 South, Long. 60 West. He remembered that this was the approximate position of Campos Buros. Tabulated by year, month and day, the columns of figures listed the elevations and compass bearings for sighting of the Echo III satellite, the latest of the huge aluminium spheres which had been orbiting the earth since Echo I was launched in 1959. Rough pencil lines had been drawn through all the entries up to the year 1968. At this point the markings became individual, each minuscule entry crossed off with a small blunt stroke. The pages were grey with the blurred graphite.

Guided by this careful patchwork of cross-hatching, Connolly found the latest entry: March 17, 1978. The time and sighting were: *6-22 a.m. Elevation 43 degrees WNW, Copella-Eridanus.* Below it was the entry for the next day, an hour later, its orientations differing slightly.

Ruefully shaking his head in admiration of Ryker's cleverness, Connolly looked at his watch. It was about 1-20, almost exactly five hours until the next traverse. Connolly glanced perfunctorily at the sky, picking out the constellation Capella, from which the satellite would emerge.

So this explained Ryker's hold over the Indians! What more impressive means had a down-and-out white man of intimidating and astonishing a tribe of primitive savages? Armed with nothing more than a set of tables and a reliable clock, he could virtually pin-point the appearance of the satellite at the first second of its visible traverse. The Indians would naturally be awed and bewildered by this phantom charioteer of the midnight sky, steadily pursuing its cosmic round, like a beacon traversing the profoundest deeps of their own unconscious. Any powers which Ryker cared to invest in the satellite would seem confirmed by his ability to control the time and place of its arrival.

Connolly realized now how the old alarm clock had told the correct time—by using his tables Ryker had read the exact time off the sky each night. A more accurate clock presumably freed him from the need to spend unnecessary time waiting for the satellite's arrival; he would now be able to set off for the tumulus only a few minutes beforehand.

Yet tonight he had gone out five hours early? Puzzling over this, Connolly noticed that the manual employed Greenwich Mean Time, and that the satellite would appear over the forest at 1-22 a.m. local time.

Backing along the pier, he began to search the sky. Away in the distance a low cry sounded into the midnight air, diffusing like a wraith over the jungle. Beside him, sitting on the bows of the launch, Connolly heard the helmsman grunt and point at the sky above the opposite bank. Following the up-raised arm, he quickly found the speeding dot of light. It was moving directly towards the tumulus, and Connolly visualized the awe and consternation that would be manifest there. Steadily the satellite crossed the sky, winking intermittently as it passed behind lanes of high-altitude cirrus, the conscripted ship of the Nambikwaras' cargo cult.

It was about to disappear among the stars in the south-east when a faint shuffling sound distracted Connolly. He looked down to find the moist-eyed youth, the son of the witch doctor, standing only a few feet away from him, regarding him dolefully.

"Hello, boy," Connolly greeted him. He pointed at the vanishing satellite. "See the star?"

The youth made a barely perceptible nod. He hesitated for a moment, his running eyes glowing like drowned moons, then stepped forward and touched Connolly's wrist-watch, tapping the dial with his horny finger nail.

Puzzled, Connolly held it up for him to inspect. The youth watched the second hand sweep around the dial, an expression of rapt and ecstatic concentration on his face. Nodding vigorously, he pointed to the sky.

Connolly grinned. "So you understand? You've rumbled old man Ryker, have you?" He nodded encouragingly to the youth, who was tapping the watch eagerly, apparently in an effort to conjure up a second satellite. Connolly began to laugh. "Sorry, boy." He slapped the manual. "What you really need is this pack of jokers."

Connolly began to walk back to the bungalow, when the

youth darted foward impulsively and blocked his way, thin legs spread widely in an aggressive stance. Then, with immense ceremony, he drew from behind his back a round painted object with a glass face that Connolly remembered he had seen him carrying before.

"That looks interesting." Connolly bent down to examine the object, caught a glimpse in the thin light of a luminous instrument dial before the youth snatched it away.

"Wait a minute, boy. Let's have another look at that."

After a pause the pantomime was repeated, but the youth was reluctant to allow Connolly more than the briefest inspection. Again Connolly saw a calibrated dial and a wavering indicator. He searched his pockets for something the youth would accept, when the latter stepped forward and touched Connolly's wrist.

Quickly Connolly unstrapped the metal chain. He tossed the watch to the youth, who instantly dropped the instrument, his barter achieved, and after a delighted yodel turned and darted off among the trees.

Bending down, careful not to touch the instrument with his hands, Connolly examined the dial. The metal housing around it was badly torn and scratched, as if the instrument had been pried from some control panel with a crude implement. But the glass face and the dial beneath it were still intact. Across the center was the legend:

LUNAR ALTIMETER
Miles: 100
GOLIATH 7
General Electric Corporation,
Schenectedy

Picking up the instrument, Connolly cradled it in his hands, for a moment feeling like Parsifal holding the Holy Grail. The pressure seals were unbroken, and the gyro bath floated freely on its air cushion. Like a graceful bird the indicator needle glided up and down the scale.

The pier creaked softly under approaching footsteps. Connolly looked up at the perspiring figure of Captain Pereira, cap in one hand, monitor dangling from the other.

"My dear Lieutenant!" he panted, "Wait till I tell you, what a farce, it's fantastic! Do you know what Ryker's doing?—it's so simple it seems unbelievable that no one's thought of it before. It's nothing short of the most magnificent practical *joke!*" Gasping, he sat down on the bale of skins leaning against the gangway. "I'll give you a clue: Narcissus."

"Echo," Connolly replied flatly, still staring at the instrument in his hands.

"You spotted it? Clever boy!" Pereira wiped his capband. "How did you guess? It wasn't that obvious." He took the manual Connolly handed him. "What the—? Ah, I see, this makes it even more clear. Of course." He slapped his knee with the manual. "You found this in his room? I take my hat off to Ryker," he continued as Connolly set the altimeter down on the pier and steadied it carefully. "Let's face it, it's something of a pretty clever trick. Can you imagine it, he comes here, finds a tribe with a strong cargo cult, opens his little manual and says 'Presto, the great white bird will be arriving: NOW!' "

Connolly nodded, then stood up, wiping his hands on a strip of rattan. When Pereira's laughter had subsided he pointed down to the glowing face of the altimeter at their feet. "Captain, something else arrived," he said quietly. "Never mind Ryker and the satellite. This cargo actually landed."

As Pereira knelt down and inspected the altimeter, whistling sharply to himself, Connolly walked over to the edge of the pier and looked out across the great back of the silent river at the giant trees which hung over the water, like forlorn mutes at some cataclysmic funeral, their thin silver voices carried away on the dead tide.

* * *

Half an hour before they set off the next morning, Connolly waited on the deck for Captain Pereira to conclude his interrogation of Ryker. The empty campong, deserted again by the Indians, basked in the heat, a single plume of smoke curling into the sky. The old witch doctor and his son had disappeared, perhaps to try their skill with a neighboring tribe, but the loss of his watch was unregretted by Connolly. Down below, safely stowed away among his baggage, was the altimeter, carefully sterilized and sealed. On the table in front of him, no more than two feet from the pistol in his belt, lay Ryker's manual.

For some reason he did not want to see Ryker, despite his contempt for him, and when Pereira emerged from the bungalow he was relieved to see that he was alone. Connolly had decided that he would not return with the search parties when they came to find the capsule; Pereira would serve adequately as a guide.

"Well?"

The Captain smiled wanly. "Oh, he admitted it, of course." He sat down on the rail, and pointed to the manual. "After all, he had no choice. Without that his existence here would be untenable."

"He admitted that Colonel Spender landed here?"

Pereira nodded. "Not in so many words, but effectively. The capsule is buried somewhere here—under the tumulus, I would guess. The Indians got hold of Colonel Spender, Ryker claims he could do nothing to help him."

"That's a lie. He saved me in the bush when the Indians thought I had landed."

With a shrug, Pereira said: "Your positions were slightly different. Besides, my impression is that Spender was dying anyway, Ryker says the parachute was badly burnt. He probably accepted a *fait accompli*, simply decided to do nothing and hush the whole thing up, incorporating the landing into the cargo cult. Very useful too. He'd been tricking the Indians with the Echo satellite, but sooner or later they would have become impatient. After the *Goliath* crashed, of course, they were prepared to go on watching the Echo and waiting for the next landing forever." A faint smile touched his lips. "It goes without saying that he regards the episode as something of a macabre joke. On you and the whole civilized world."

A door slammed on the veranda, and Ryker stepped out into the sunlight. Bare-chested and hatless, he strode towards the launch.

"Connolly," he called down, "you've got my book of tricks there!"

Connolly reached forward and fingered the manual, the butt of his pistol tapping the table edge. He looked up at Ryker, at his big golden frame bathed in the morning light. Despite his still belligerent tone, a subtle change had come over Ryker. The ironic gleam in his eye had gone, and the inner core of wariness and suspicion which had warped the man and exiled him from the world was now visible. Connolly realized that, curiously, their respective roles had been reversed. He remembered Pereira reminding him that the Indians were at equilibrium with their environment, accepting its constraints and never seeking to dominate the towering arbors of the forest, in a sense an externalization of their own unconscious phyches. Ryker had upset that equilibrium, and by using the Echo satellite had brought the 20th century and its psychopathic projections into the heart of the Amazonian deep, transforming the Indians into a community of superstitious and materialistic sightseers, their whole culture oriented around the mythical god of the puppet star. It was Connolly who now accepted the jungle for what it was, acknowledging its fatalism and implacable indifference, seeing himself and the abortive space-flight in this fresh perspective, where tragedy and triumph were equally vainglorious.

Pereira gestured to the helmsman, and with a muffled roar the engine started. The launch pulled lightly against its lines.

"Connolly!" Ryker's voice was shriller now, his bellicose shout overlayed by a higher note. For a moment the two men looked at each other, and in the wavering, almost craven eyes above him Connolly glimpsed the helpless isolation of Ryker, his futile attempt to impose his will on the forest.

Picking up the manual, Connolly leaned forward and tossed it through the air on to the pier. Ryker tried to catch it, then knelt down and picked it up before it slipped through the springing poles. Still kneeling, he watched as the lines were cast off and the launch surged ahead.

They moved out into the channel and plunged through the bowers of spray into the heavier swells of the open current.

As they reached a sheltering bend and the somber figure of Ryker faded for the last time among the creepers and sunlight, Connolly turned to Pereira. "Captain—what actually happened to Colonel Spender? You said the Indians wouldn't eat a white man."

"They eat their gods," Pereira said.

ESCAPEMENT

NEITHER OF US was watching the play too closely when I first noticed the slip. I was stretched back in front of the fire with the cross-word, braising gently and toying with 17 down ("told by antique clocks?: 5, 5.") while Helen was hemming an old petticoat, looking up only when the third lead, a heavy-chinned youth with a 42-inch neck and a base-surge voice, heaved manfully downscreen. The play was "My Sons, My Sons," one of those Thursday night melodramas Channel 2 put out through the winter months, and had been running for about an hour; we'd reached that ebb somewhere round Act 3 Scene 3 just after the old farmer learns that his sons no longer respect him. The whole play must have been recorded on film, and it sounded extremely funny to switch from the old man's broken mutterings back to the showdown sequence fifteen minutes earlier when the eldest son starts drumming his chest and dragging in the high symbols. Somewhere an engineer was out of a job.

"They've got their reels crossed," I told Helen. "This is where we came in."

"Is it?" she said, looking up. "I wasn't watching. Tap the set."

"Just wait and see. In a moment everyone in the studio will start apologising."

Helen peered at the screen. "I don't think we've seen this," she said. "I'm sure we haven't. Quiet."

I shrugged and went back to 17 down, thinking vaguely about sand dials and water clocks. The scene dragged on; the old man stood his ground, ranted over his turnips and thundered desperately for Ma. The studio must have decided to run it straight through again and pretend no-one had noticed. Even so they'd be fifteen minutes behind their schedule.

Ten minutes later it happened again.

I sat up. "That's funny," I said slowly. "Haven't they spotted it yet? They can't all be asleep."

"What's the matter?" Helen asked, looking up from her needle basket. "Is something wrong with the set?"

"I thought you were watching. I told you we'd seen this before. Now they're playing it back for the third time."

"They're not," Helen insisted. "I'm sure they aren't. You must have read the book."

"Heaven forbid." I watched the set closely. Any minute now an announcer spitting on a sandwich would splutter red-faced to the screen. I'm not one of those people who reach for their phones every time someone mispronounces meteorology, but this time I knew there'd be thousands who'd feel it their duty to keep the studio exchanges blocked all night. And for any go-ahead comedian on a rival station the lapse was a god-send.

"Do you mind if I change the programme?" I asked Helen. "See if anything else is on."

"Don't. This is the most interesting part of the play. You'll spoil it."

"Darling, you're not even watching. I'll come back to it in a moment, I promise."

On Channel 5 a panel of three professors and a chorus girl were staring hard at a Roman pot. The question-master, a suave-voiced Oxford don, kept up a lot of cozy patter about scraping the bottom of the barrow. The professors seemed stumped, but the girl looked as if she knew exactly what went into the pot but didn't dare say it.

On 9 there was a lot of studio laughter and someone was giving a sports-car to an enormous woman in a cartwheel hat. The woman nervously ducked her head away from the camera and stared glumly at the car. The compére opened the door for her and I was wondering whether she'd try to get into it when Helen cut in:

"Harry, don't be mean. You're just playing."

I turned back to the play on Channel 2. The same scene was on, nearing the end of its run.

"Now watch it," I told Helen. She usually managed to catch on the third time round. "Put that sewing away, it's getting on my nerves. God, I know this off by heart."

"Sh!" Helen told me. "Can't you stop talking?"

I lit a cigarette and lay back in the sofa, waiting. The apologies, to say the least, would have to be magniloquent. Two ghost runs at £100 a minute totted up to a tidy heap of dubloons.

The scene drew to a close, the old man stared heavily at his boots, the dusk drew down and—

We were back where we started from.

"Fantastic!" I said, standing up and turning some snow off the screen. "It's incredible."

"I didn't know you enjoyed this sort of play," Helen said calmly. "You never used to." She glanced over at the screen and then went back to her petticoat.

I watched her warily. A million years earlier I'd probably have run howling out of the cave and flung myself thankfully under the nearest dinosaur. Nothing in the meanwhile had lessened the dangers hemming in the undaunted husband.

"Darling," I explained patiently, just keeping the edge out of my voice, "in case you hadn't noticed they are now playing this same scene through for the fourth time."

"The fourth time?" Helen said doubtfully. "Are they repeating it?"

I was visualising a studio full of announcers and engineers slumped unconscious over their mikes and valves, while an automatic camera pumped out the same reel. Eerie but unlikely. There were monitor receivers as well as the critics, agents, sponsors, and, unforgivably, the playwright himself weighting every minute and every word in their private currencies. They'd all have a lot to say under tomorrow's head-lines.

"Sit down and stop fidgetting," Helen said. "Have you lost your bone?"

I felt round the cushions and ran my hand along the carpet below the sofa.

"My cigarette," I said. "I must have thrown it into the fire. I don't think I dropped it."

I turned back to the set and switched on the give-away programme, noting the time, 9.03, so that I could get back to Channel 2 at 9.15. When the explanation came I just had to hear it.

"I thought you were enjoying the play," Helen said. "Why've you turned it off?"

I gave her what sometimes passes in our flat for a withering frown and settled back.

The enormous woman was still at it in front of the cameras, working her way up a pyramid of questions on cookery. The audience was subdued but interest mounted. Eventually she answered the jackpot question and the audience roared and thumped their seats like a lot of madmen. The compére led her across the stage to another sports car.

"She'll have a stable of them soon," I said aside to Helen.

The woman shook hands and awkwardly dipped the brim of her hat, smiling nervously with embarrassment.

The gesture was oddly familiar.

I jumped up and switched to Channel 5. The panel were still staring hard at their pot.

Then I started to realise what was going on.

All three programmes were repeating themselves.

"Helen," I said over my shoulder. "Get me a scotch and soda, will you?"

"What *is* the matter? Have you strained your back?"

"Quickly, quickly!" I snapped my fingers.

"Hold on." She got up and went into the pantry.

I looked at the time. 9-12. Then I returned to the play and kept my eyes glued to the screen. Helen came back and put something down on the end-table.

"There you are. You all right?"

When it switched I thought I was ready for it, but the surprise must have knocked me flat. I found myself lying out on the sofa. The first thing I did was reach round for the drink.

"Where did you put it?" I asked Helen.

"What?"

"The Scotch. You brought it in a couple of minutes ago. It was on the table."

"You've been dreaming," she said gently. She leant forward and started watching the play.

I went into the pantry and found the bottle. As I filled a tumbler I noticed the clock over the kitchen sink. 9-07. An hour slow, now that I thought about it. But my wrist-watch said 9-05, and always ran perfectly. And the clock on the mantelpiece in the lounge also said 9-05.

Before I really started worrying I had to make sure.

Mullvaney, our neighbour in the flat above, opened his door when I knocked.

"Hello, Bartley. Corkscrew?"

"No, no," I told him. "What's the right time? Our clocks are going crazy."

He glanced at his wrist. "Nearly ten past."

"Nine or ten?"

He looked at his watch again. "Nine, should be. What's up?"

"I don't know whether I'm losing my—" I started to say. Then I stopped.

Mullvaney eyed me curiously. Over his shoulder I heard a wave of studio applause, broken by the creamy, unctuous voice of the give-away compére.

"How long's that programme been on?" I asked him.

"About twenty minutes. Aren't you watching?"

"No," I said, adding casually. "Is anything wrong with your set?"

He shook his head. "Nothing. Why?"

"Mine's chasing its tail. Anyway, thanks."

"OK," he said. He watched me go down the stairs and shrugged as he shut his door.

I went into the hall, picked up the phone and dialled.

"Hello, Tom?" Tom Farnold works the desk next to mine at the office. "Tom, Harry here. What time do you make it?"

"Time the liberals were back."

"No, seriously."

"Let's see. Twelve past nine. By the way, did you find those pickles I left for you in the safe?"

"Yeah, thanks. Listen, Tom," I went on, "the goddamdest things are happening here. We were watching Diller's play on Channel 2 when—"

"I'm watching it now. Hurry it up."

"You are? Well, how do you explain this repetition business? And the way the clocks are stuck between 9 and 9-15?"

Tom laughed. "I don't know," he said. "I suggest you go outside and give the house a shake."

I reached out for the glass I had with me on the hall table, wondering how to explain to—

The next moment I found myself back on the sofa. I was holding the newspaper and looking at 17 down. A part of my mind was thinking about antique clocks.

I pulled myself out of it and glanced across at Helen. She was sitting quietly with her needle basket. The all too familiar play was repeating itself and by the clock on the mantelpiece it was still just after 9.

I went back into the hall and dialled Tom again, trying not to stampede myself. In some way, I hadn't begun to understand how, a section of time was spinning round in a circle, with myself in the centre.

"Tom," I asked quickly as soon as he picked up the phone. "Did I call you five minutes ago?"

"Who's that again?"

"Harry here. Harry Bartley. Sorry Tom." I paused and rephrased the question, trying to make it sound intelligible. "Tom, did you phone me up about five minutes ago? We've had a little trouble with the line here."

"No," he told me. "Wasn't me. By the way, did you get those pickles I left in the safe?"

"Thanks a lot," I said, beginning to panic. "Are you watching the play, Tom?"

"Yes. I think I'll get back to it. See you."

I went into the kitchen and had a long close look at myself in the mirror. A crack across it dropped one side of my face three inches below the other, but apart from that I couldn't see anything that added up to a psychosis. My eyes seemed steady, pulse was in the low seventies, no tics or clammy traumatic sweat. Everything around me seemed much too solid and authentic for a dream.

I waited for a minute and then went back to the lounge and sat down. Helen was watching the play.

I leant forward and turned the knob round. The picture dimmed and swayed off.

"Harry, I'm watching that! Don't switch it off."

I went over to her. "Poppet," I said, holding my voice together. "Listen to me, please. Very carefully. It's important."

She frowned, put her sewing down and took my hands.

"For some reason, I don't know why, we seem to be in a sort of circular time trap, just going round and round. You're not aware of it, and I can't find anyone else who is either."

Helen stared at me in amazement. "Harry," she started, "what are you—"

"Helen!" I insisted, gripping her shoulders. "Listen! For the last two hours a section of time about 15 minutes long has been repeating itself. The clocks are stuck between 9 and 9-15. That play you're watching has——"

"Harry, darling." She looked at me and smiled helplessly. "You are silly. Now turn it on again."

I gave up.

As I switched the set on I ran through all the other channels just to see if anything had changed.

The panel stared at their pot, the fat woman won her sports car, the old farmer ranted. On Channel 1, the old BBC service which put out a couple of hours on alternate evenings, two newspaper men were interviewing a scientific pundit who appeared on popular educational programmes.

"What effect these dense eruptions of gas will have so far it's impossible to tell. However, there's certainly no cause for any alarm. These billows have mass, and I think we can expect a lot of strange optical effects as the light leaving the sun is deflected by them gravitationally."

He started playing with a set of coloured celluloid balls running on concentric metal rings, and fiddling with a ripple tank mounted against a mirror on the table.

One of the newsmen asked: "What about the relationship between light and time? If I remember my relativity they're tied up together pretty closely. Are you sure we won't all need to add another hand to our clocks and watches?"

The pundit smiled. "I think we'll be able to get along without that. Time is extremely complicated, but I can assure you the clocks won't suddenly start running backwards or sideways."

I listened to him until Helen began to remonstrate. I switched the play on for her and went off into the hall. The fool didn't know what he was talking about. What I couldn't understand was why I was the only person who realized what was going on. If I could get Tom over I might just be able to convince him.

I picked up the phone and glanced at my watch.

9-13. By the time I got through to Tom the next change-over would be due. Somehow I didn't like the idea of being picked up and flung to the sofa, however painless it might be. I put the phone down and went into the lounge.

The jump-back was smoother than I expected. I wasn't conscious of anything, not even the slightest tremor. A phrase was stuck in my mind: Olden Times.

The newspaper was back on my lap, folded around the cross-word. I looked through the clues.

17 down: Told by antique clocks? 5, 5.

I must have solved it sub-consciously.

I remembered that I'd intended to phone Tom.

"Hullo, Tom?" I asked when I got through. "Harry here."

"Did you get those pickles I left in the safe?"

"Yes, thanks a lot. Tom, could you come round tonight? Sorry to ask you this late, but it's fairly urgent."

"Yes, of course," he said. "What's the trouble?"

"I'll tell you when you get here. As soon as you can?"

"Sure. I'll leave right away. Is Helen all right?"

"Yes, she's fine. Thanks again."

I went into the dining-room and pulled a bottle of gin and a couple of tonics out of the sideboard. He'd need a drink when he heard what I had to say.

Then I realized he'd never make it. From Earls Court it would take him at least half an hour to reach us at Maida Vale and he'd probably get no further than Marble Arch.

I filled my glass out of the virtually bottomless bottle of Scotch and tried to work out a plan of action.

The first step was to get hold of someone like myself who retained his awareness of the past switch-backs. Somewhere else there must be others trapped in their little 15-minute cages who were also wondering desperately how to get out. I could start by phoning everyone I knew and then going on at random through the phone-book. But what could we do if we did find each other? In fact there was nothing to do except sit tight and wait for it all to wear off. At least I knew I wasn't looping my loop. Once these billows or whatever they were had burnt themselves out we'd be able to get off the round-about.

Until then I had an unlimited supply of whisky waiting for me in the half-empty bottle standing on the sink, though of course there was one snag: I'd never be able to get drunk.

I was musing round some of the other possibilities available and wondering how to get a permanent record of what was going on when an idea hit me.

I got out the phone-directory and looked up the number of KBC-TV, Channel 9.

A girl at reception answered the phone. After haggling with her for a couple of minutes I persuaded her to put me through to one of the producers.

"Hullo," I said. "Is the jack-pot question in to-night's programme known to any members of the studio audience?"

"No, of course not."

"I see. As a matter of interest, do you yourself know it?"

"No," he said. "All the questions to-night are known only to our senior programme producer and M. Phillipe Soisson of Savoy Hotels Limited. They're a closely guarded secret."

"Thanks," I said. "If you've got a piece of paper handy I'll give you the jack-pot question. 'List the complete menu at the Guildhall Coronation Banquet in July 1953.'"

There were muttered consultations, and a second voice came through.

"Who's that speaking?"

"Mr. H. R. Bartley, 129b Sutton Court Road, N.W.—"

Before I could finish I found myself back in the lounge.

The jump-back had caught me. But instead of being stretched out on the sofa I was standing up, leaning on one elbow against the mantelpiece, looking down at the newspaper.

My eyes were focussed clearly on the cross-word puzzle, and before I pulled them away and started thinking over my call to the studio I noticed something that nearly dropped me into the grate.

17 down had been filled in.

I picked up the paper and showed it to Helen.

"Did you do this clue? 17 down?"

"No," she said. "I never even look at the cross-word."

The clock on the mantelpiece caught my eye, and I forgot about the studio and playing tricks with other people's time.

9-03.

The merry-go-round was closing in. I thought the jump-back had come sooner than I expected. At least two minutes earlier, somewhere round 9-13.

And not only was the repetition interval getting shorter, but as the arc edged inwards on itself it was uncovering the real time stream running below it, the stream in which the other I, unknown to myself here, had solved the clue, stood up, walked over to the mantelpiece and filled in 17 down.

I sat down on the sofa, watching the clock carefully.

For the first time that evening Helen was thumbing over the pages of a magazine. The work-basket was tucked away on the bottom shelf of the bookcase.

"Do you want this on any longer?" she asked me. "It's not very good."

I turned to the panel game. The three professors and the chorus girl were still playing around with their pot.

On Channel 1 the pundit was sitting at the table with his models.

". . . alarm. These billows have mass, and I think we can expect a lot of strange optical effects as the light—"

I switched it off.

The next jump-back came at 9-11. Somewhere I'd left the mantelpiece, gone back to the sofa and lit a cigarette.

It was 9-04. Helen had opened the verandah windows and was looking out into the street.

The set was on again so I pulled the plug out at the main. I threw the cigarette into the fire; not having seen myself light it, made it taste like someone else's.

"Harry, like to go out for a stroll?" Helen suggested. "It'll be rather nice in the park."

Each successive jump-back gave us a new departure point. If now I bundled her outside and got her down to the end of the road, at the next jump we'd both be back in the lounge again, but probably have decided to drive to the pub instead.

"Harry?"

"What, sorry?"

"Are you asleep, angel? Like to go for a walk? It'll wake you up."

"All right," I said. "Go and get your coat."

"Will you be warm enough like that?"

She went off into the bedroom.

I walked round the lounge and convinced myself that I was awake. The shadows, the solid feel of the chairs, the definition was much too fine for a dream.

It was 9-08. Normally Helen would take ten minutes to put on her coat.

The jump-back came almost immediately.

It was 9-06.

I was still on the sofa and Helen was bending down and picking up her work basket.

This time, at last, the set was off.

"Have you got any money on you?" Helen asked.

I felt in my pocket automatically. "Yes. How much do you want?"

Helen looked at me. "Well, what do you usually pay for the drinks? We'll only have a couple."

"We're going to the pub, are we?"

"Darling, are you all right?" She came over to me. "You look all strangled. Is that shirt too tight?"

"Helen," I said, getting up. "I've got to try to explain something to you. I don't know why it's happening, it's something to do with these billows of gas the sun's releasing."

Helen was watching me with her mouth open.

"Harry," she started to say nervously. "What's the matter?"

"I'm quite all right," I assured her. "It's just that everything is happening very rapidly and I don't think there's much time left."

I kept on glancing at the clock and Helen followed my

eyes to it and went over to the mantelpiece. Watching me
he moved it round and I heard the pendulum jangle.

"No, no," I shouted. I grabbed it and pushed it back
against the wall.

We jumped back to 9-07.

Helen was in the bedroom. I had exactly a minute left.

"Harry," she called. "Darling, do you want to, or don't you?"

I was by the lounge window, muttering something.

I was out of touch with what my real self was doing in
the normal time channel. The Helen talking to me now was
a phantom.

It was I, not Helen and everybody else, who was riding
the merry-go-round.

Jump.

9-07.15

Helen was standing in the doorway.

". . . down to the . . . the . . ." I was saying.

Helen watched me, frozen. A fraction of a minute left.

I started to walk over to her.

to walk over to her

ver to her

er

I came out of it like a man catapulted from a revolving
door. I was stretched out flat on the sofa, a hard aching pain
running from the top of my head down past my right ear
into my neck.

I looked at the time. 9-45. I could hear Helen moving
around in the dining-room. I lay there, steadying the room
round me, and in a few minutes she came in carrying a tray
and a couple of glasses.

"How do you feel?" she asked, making up an alka-seltzer.
I let it fizzle down and drank it.

"What happened?" I asked. "Did I collapse?"

"Not exactly. You were watching the play. I thought you
looked rather seedy so I suggested we go out for a drink. You
went into a sort of convulsion."

I stood up slowly and rubbed my neck. "God, I didn't
dream all that! I couldn't have done."

"What was it about?"

"A sort of crazy merry-go-round—" The pain grabbed at
my neck when I spoke. I went over to the set and switched
it on. "Hard to explain coherently. Time was—" I flinched
as the pain bit in again.

"Sit down and rest," Helen said. "I'll come and join you.
Like a drink?"

"Thanks. A big Scotch."

I looked at the set. On Channel 1 there was a breakdown

sign, a cabaret on 2, a flood-lit stadium on 5, and a variety show on 9. No sign anywhere of either Diller's play or the panel game.

Helen brought the drink in and sat down on the sofa with me.

"It started off when we were watching the play," I explained, massaging my neck.

"Sh, don't bother now. Just relax."

I put my head on Helen's shoulder and looked up at the ceiling, listening to the sound coming from the variety show. I thought back through each turn of the round-about, wondering whether I could have dreamt it all.

Ten minutes later Helen said, "Well, I didn't think much of that. And they're doing an encore. Good heavens."

"Who are?" I asked. I watched the light from the screen flicker across her face.

"That team of acrobats. The something Brothers. One of them even slipped. How do you feel?"

"Fine." I turned my head round and looked at the screen.

Three or four acrobats with huge v-torsos and skin briefs were doing simple handstands onto each other's arms. They finished the act and went into a more involved routine, throwing around a girl in leopard skin panties. The applause was deafening. I thought they were moderately good.

Two of them began to give what seemed to be a demonstration of dynamic tension, straining against each other like a pair of catatonic bulls, their necks and legs locked, until one of them was levered slowly off the ground.

"Why do they keep on doing that?" Helen said. "They've done it twice already."

"I don't think they have," I said. "This is a slightly different act."

The pivot man tremored, one of his huge banks of muscles collapsed, and the whole act toppled and then sprung apart.

"They slipped there the last time," Helen said.

"No, no," I pointed out quickly. "That one was a headstand. Here they were stretched out horizontally."

"You weren't watching," Helen told me. She leant forward. "Well, what are they playing at? They're repeating the whole thing for the third time."

It was an entirely new act to me, but I didn't try to argue. I sat up and looked at the clock.

10-05.

"Darling," I said, putting my arm round her. "Hold tight."

"What do you mean?"

"This is the merry-go-round. And you're driving."

THE THOUSAND DREAMS
OF STELLAVISTA

No-one ever comes to Vermilion Sands now, and I suppose there are few people who have ever heard of it, but ten years ago, when Fay and I first went to live at 99 Stellavista, just before our marriage broke up, the colony was still remembered as the one-time playground of movie czars, delinquent heiresses and eccentric cosmopolites in those fabulous years before the Recess. Admittedly most of the abstract villas and fake palazzos were empty, their huge gardens overgrown, two-level swimming pools long drained, and the whole place was degenerating like an abandoned amusement park, but there was enough bizarre extravagance in the air to make one realize that the giants had only just departed.

I remember the day we first drove down Stellavista in the property agent's car, and how exhilarated Fay and I were, despite our bogus front of bourgeois respectability. Fay, I think, was even a little awed—one or two of the big names were living on behind the shuttered terraces—and we must have been the easiest prospects the young agent had seen for months.

Presumably this was why he tried to work off the really weird places first. The half dozen we saw to begin with were obviously the old regulars, faithfully paraded in the hope that some unwary client might be staggered into buying one of them, or failing that, temporarily lose all standards of comparison and take the first tolerably conventional pile to come along.

One, just off Stellavista and M, would have shaken even an old-guard surrealist on a heroin swing. Screened from the road by a mass of dusty rhododendrons, it consisted of six huge aluminium-shelled spheres suspended like the elements of a mobile from an enormous concrete davit. The largest sphere contained the lounge, the others, successively smaller and spiralling upward into the air, the bedrooms and kitchen. Many of the hull plates had been holed, and the entire slightly tarnished structure hung down into the weeds poking through the cracked concrete court like a collection of forgotten space-ships in a vacant lot.

Stamers, the agent, left us sitting in the car, partly shielded by the rhododendrons, ran across to the entrance and switched the place on (all the houses in Vermilion Sands, it goes without saying, were psychotropic). There was a dim whirring, and the spheres tipped and began to rotate, brushing against the undergrowth.

Fay sat in the car, staring up in amazement at this awful, beautiful thing, but out of curiosity I got out and walked over to the entrance, the main sphere slowing as I approached, uncertainly steering a course toward me, the smaller ones following.

According to the descriptive brochure, the house had been built eight years earlier for a TV mogul as a weekend retreat. The pedigree was a long one, through two movie starlets, a psychiatrist, an ultrasonic composer (the late Dmitri Shochmann—a notorious madman, I remembered that he invited a score of guests to his suicide party, but no-one had turned up to watch. Chagrined, he bungled the attempt) and an automobile stylist. With such an overlay of more or less blue-chip responses built into it, the house should have been snapped up within a week, even in Vermilion Sands; to have been on the market for several months, if not years, indicated that the previous tenants had been none too happy there.

Ten feet from me, the main sphere hovered uncertainly, the entrance extending downwards. Stamers stood in the open doorway, smiling encouragingly, but the house seemed nervous of something. As I stepped forward it suddenly jerked away, almost in alarm, the entrance retracting and sending a low shudder through the rest of the spheres.

It's always interesting to watch a psychotropic house try to adjust itself to strangers, particularly those at all guarded or suspicious. The responses vary, a blend of past reactions to negative emotions, the hostility of the previous tenants, a traumatic encounter with a bailiff or burglar (though both these usually stay well away from PT houses; the dangers of an inverting balcony or the sudden deflatus of a corridor are too great). The initial reaction can be a surer indication of a house's true condition than any amount of sales talk about horse-power and moduli of elasticity.

This one was definitely on the defensive. When I climbed up onto the entrance Stamers was fiddling desperately with the control console recessed into the wall behind the door, damping the volume down as low as possible. Usually a property agent will select medium/full, trying to heighten the PT responses.

He smiled thinly at me. "Circuits are a little worn. Nothing serious, we'll replace them on contract. Some of the previous owners were show business people, had an oversimplified view of the full life."

I nodded, walking through onto the balcony which ringed the wide sunken lounge. It was a beautiful room all right, with opaque plastex walls and white fluo-glass ceiling, but something terrible had happened there. As it responded to me, the ceiling lifting slightly and the walls growing less opaque, reflecting my perspective-seeking eye, I noticed that curious mottled knots were forming, indicating where the room had been strained and healed faultily. Deep hidden rifts began to distort the sphere, ballooning out one of the alcoves like a bubble of over-extended gum.

Stamers tapped my elbow.

"Lively responses, aren't they, Mr. Talbot?" He put his hand on the wall behind us. The plastex swam and whirled like boiling toothpaste, then extruded itself into a small ledge. Stamers sat down on the lip, which quickly expanded to match the contours of his body, providing back and arm rests. "Sit down and relax, Mr. Talbot, let yourself feel at home here."

The seat cushioned up around me like an enormous white hand, and immediately the walls and ceiling quietened—obviously Stamers' first job was to get his clients off their feet before their restless shuffling could do any damage. Someone living there must have put in a lot of anguished pacing and knuckle-cracking.

"Of course, you're getting nothing but custom-built units here," Stamers said. "The vinyl chains in this plastex were hand-crafted literally molecule by molecule."

I felt the room shift around me. The ceiling was dilating and contracting in steady pulses, an absurdly exaggerated response to our own respiratory rhythms, but the motions were overlayed by sharp transverse spasms, feed-back from some cardiac ailment.

The house was not only frightened of us, it was seriously ill. Somebody, Dmitri Shochmann perhaps, overflowing with self-hate, had committed an appalling injury to himself, and the house was recapitulating its previous response. I was about to ask Stamers if the suicide party had been staged here when he sat up and looked around fretfully.

At the same time my ears started to sing. Mysteriously,

the air pressure inside the lounge was building up, gusts of old grit whirling out into the hallway towards the exit.

Stamers was on his feet, the seat telescoping back into the wall.

"Er, Mr. Talbot, let's stroll around the garden, give you the feel of—"

He broke off, face creased in alarm. The ceiling was only five feet above our heads, contracting like a huge white bladder.

"—explosive decompression," Stamers finished automatically, taking my arm quickly. "I don't understand this," he muttered as we ran out into the hallway, the air whooshing past us.

I had a shrewd idea what was happening, and sure enough we found Fay peering into the control console, swinging the volume tabs.

Stamers dived past her. We were almost dragged back into the lounge as the ceiling began its outward leg and sucked the air in through the doorway, but just in time he reached the emergency panel and switched the house off.

Wide-eyed, he buttoned his shirt up, nodding to Fay. "That was close, Mrs. Talbot, that was really close." He gave a light hysterical laugh.

As we walked back to the car, the giant spheres resting among the weeds, he said: "Well, Mr. Talbot, it's a fine property. A remarkable pedigree for a house only eight years old. An exciting challenge, you know, a new dimension in living."

I gave him a weak smile. "Maybe, but it's not exactly *us*, is it?"

We had come to Vermilion Sands for two years, while I opened a law office in downtown Red Beach twenty miles away. Apart from the dust, smog and inflationary prices of real estate in Red Beach, a strong motive for coming out to Vermilion Sands was that any number of potential clients were mouldering away there in the old mansions—forgotten movie queens, lonely impresarios and the like, some of the most litigious people in the world. Once installed, I could make my rounds of the bridge tables and dinner parties, tactfully stimulating a little righteous will-paring and contract-breaking.

However, as we drove down Stellavista on our inspection tour I wondered if we'd find anywhere suitable. Rapidly we went through a mock Assyrian ziggurat (the last owner had suffered from St. Vitus's Dance, and the whole structure still jittered like a galvanized Tower of Pisa), and a con-

verted submarine pen (here the problem had been alcoholism, we could *feel* the gloom and helplessness come down off
those huge damp walls soaring up into the darkness).

Finally Stamers gave up and brought us back to earth.
Unfortunately his more conventional properties were little
better. The real trouble was that most of Vermilion Sands is
composed of early, or primitive-fantastic, period psychotropic, when the possibilities offered by the new bio-plastic
medium rather went to architects' heads. It was some years
before a compromise was reached between the 100% respon-
sive structure and the rigid non-responsive houses of the past.
The first PT houses had so many senso-cells distributed over
them, echoing every shift of mood and position of the occupants, that living in one was like inhabiting someone else's
brain.

Unluckily bioplastics need a lot of exercise or they grow
rigid and crack, and many people believe that PT buildings
are still given unnecessarily subtle memories and are far too
sensitive—there's the apocryphal story of the millionaire of
plebian origins who was literally frozen out of a million-
dollar mansion he had bought from an aristocratic family.
The place had been trained to respond to their habitual
rudeness and bad temper, and reacted discordantly when
re-adjusting itself to the millionaire, unintentionally parody-
ing his soft-spoken politeness.

But although the echoes of previous tenants can be intru-
sive, this naturally has its advantages. Many medium-priced
PT homes resonate with the bygone laughter of happy families, the relaxed harmony of a successful marriage. It was
something like this that I wanted for Fay and myself. In
the previous year our relationship had begun to fade a little,
and a really well-integrated house with a healthy set of re-
flexes—say, those of a prosperous bank president and his
devoted spouse—would go a long way towards healing the
rifts between us.

Leafing through the brochures when we reached the end
of Stellavista I could see that domesticated bank presidents
had been in short supply at Vermilion Sands. The pedigrees
were either packed with ulcer-ridden, quadri-divorced TV
executives, or discreetly blank.

99 Stellavista was in the latter category. As we climbed
out of the car and walked up the short drive I searched the
pedigree for data on the past tenants, but only the original
owner was given: a Miss Emma Slack, psychic orientation un-
stated.

That it was a woman's house was obvious. Shaped like an enormous orchid, it was set back on a low concrete dais in the center of a trim blue gravel court, the white plastex wings, which carried the lounge on one side and the master bedroom on the other, spanning out across the magnolias on the far side of the drive. Between the two wings, on the first floor, was an open terrace around a small heart-shaped swimpool. The terrace ran back to the central bulb, a three-story segment containing the chauffeur's apartment and a vast two-decker kitchen.

The house seemed to be in good condition. While we parked I looked up at the white wings fanning out above us, and the plastex was unscarred, its thin seams running smoothly to the far rim like the veins of a giant leaf.

Curiously, Stamers was in no hurry to switch on. He pointed to left and right as we made our way up the glass staircase to the terrace, underlining various attractive features, but made no effort to find the control console, and I suspected that the house might be a static conversion—a fair number of PT houses are frozen in one or other position at the end of their working lives, and make tolerable static homes.

"It's not bad," I admitted, looking out across the powder-blue water as Stamers piled on the superlatives. Through the glass bottom of the pool the car parked below loomed like a colored whale asleep on the ocean bed. "This is the sort of thing, all right. But what about switching it on?"

Stamers stepped around me and headed off after Fay. "You'll want to see the kitchen first, Mr. Talbot. There's no hurry, let yourself feel at home here."

The kitchen was fabulous, banks of gleaming control panels and auto units. Everything was recessed and stylized, blending into the over-all color scheme, complex gadgets folding back into self-sealing cabinets. Boiling an egg there would have taken me a couple of days.

"Quite a plant," I commented. Fay wandered around in a daze of delight, automatically fingering the chrome. "Looks as if it's tooled up to produce penicillin." I tapped the brochure. "But why so cheap? At 25 thousand it's damn nearly being given away."

Stamers' eyes brightened. He flashed me a broad conspiratorial smile which indicated that this was *my* year, *my* day. Taking me off on a tour of the rumpus room and library, he began to hammer home the merits of the house, extolling his company's 35-year easy-purchase plan (they wanted anything except cash—there was no money in that) and the beauty and simplicity of the garden (mostly flexible polyurethane perennials).

Finally, apparently convinced that I was sold, he switched the house on.

Well, I didn't know then what it was, but something strange had taken place in that house. Emma Slack had certainly been a woman with a powerful and oblique personality. As I walked slowly around the empty lounge, feeling the walls angle and edge away, doorways widen when I approached, curious echoes stirred through the memories embedded in the house. The responses were undefined, but somehow eerie and unsettling, like being continually watched over one's shoulder, each room adjusting itself to my soft random footsteps as if they contained the possibility of some explosive burst of passion or temperament.

Inclining my head, however, I seemed to hear other echoes, delicate and feminine, a graceful swirl of movement reflected in a brief fluid sweep in one corner, the decorous unfolding of an archway or recess.

Then, abruptly, the mood would invert, and the hollow eerieness return.

Fay touched my arm. "Howard, it's strange."

I shrugged. "Interesting, though. Remember, our own responses will overlay these within a few days."

Fay shook her head. "I couldn't stand it, Howard. Mr. Stamers must have something normal."

"Darling, Vermilion Sands is Vermilion Sands. Don't expect to find the suburban norms. People here were individualists."

I looked down at Fay. Her small oval face, with its child-like mouth and chin, the fringe of blond hair and pert nose, seemed lost and anxious, and I realized that Fay was just a suburban housewife who felt out of place trying to live up to the exotic flora of Vermilion Sands.

I put my arm around her shoulder. "O.K., sweetie, you're quite right. Let's find somewhere we can put our feet up and relax, be ourselves. Now, what are we going to say to Stamers?"

Surprisingly, Stamers didn't seem all that disappointed. When I shook my head he put up a token protest but soon gave in and switched off the house.

"I know how Mrs. Talbot feels," he conceded as we went down the staircase. "Some of these places have got too much personality built into them. Living with someone like Gloria Tremayne isn't too easy."

I stopped, two steps from the bottom, a curious ripple of recognition running through my mind.

"Gloria Tremayne? I thought the only owner was a Miss Emma Slack."

Stamers nodded. "Yeah. Gloria Tremayne. Emma Slack was her real name. Don't say I told you, though everybody living around here knows it. We keep it quiet as long as we can. If we said Gloria Tremayne no-one would even look at the place."

"Gloria Tremayne," Fay repeated, puzzled. "She was the movie star who shot her husband, wasn't she? He was a famous architect—Howard, weren't you on that case?"

As Fay's voice chattered on I turned and looked up the staircase towards the sun-lounge, my mind casting itself back ten years to one of the most famous trials of the decade, whose course and verdict were as much as anything else to mark the end of a whole generation, and show up the irresponsibilities of the world before the Recess. Even though Gloria Tremayne had been acquitted, everyone knew that she had cold-bloodedly murdered her husband, the architect Miles Vanden Starr, as he lay asleep, and only the silver-tongued pleading of Daniel Hammett, her defense attorney, assisted by a young man called Howard Talbot, had saved her. I said to Fay: "Yes, I helped to defend her. It seems a long time ago. Angel, you wait in the car. I want to check something."

Before she could follow me I ran up the staircase onto the terrace and closed the glass double doors behind me. Inert and unresponsive now, the white walls rose into the sky on either side of the pool. The water was motionless, a transparent block of condensed time, through which I could see the drowned images of Fay and Stamers sitting in the car, for a moment, as I thought of Gloria Tremayne, like an embalmed fragment of my future.

For three weeks, during her trial ten years earlier, I sat only a few feet from Gloria Tremayne, and like everyone else in that crowded courtroom I would never forget her cool mask-like face, the composed eyes that examined each of the witnesses as they gave their testimony—chauffeur, police surgeon, neighbors who heard the shots—like a brilliant spider arraigned by its victims, never once showing any emotion or response. As they dismembered her web, skein by skein, she sat impassively at its center, giving Hammett no encouragement, content to repose in the image of herself ("The Ice Face") projected across the globe for the previous 15 years.

Perhaps in the end this saved her, the jury unable to out-stare the enigma. To be honest, by the last week of the trial I had lost all interest in it. As I steered Hammett through his brief, opening and shutting his red wooden suitcase (the Hammett hallmark, it was an excellent jury distractor) whenever he indicated, my attention was fixed completely on Gloria Tremayne, trying to find some flaw in the mask through which I could glimpse her personality. I suppose that I was just another naive young man who had fallen in love with a myth manufactured by a thousand publicity agents, but for me the sensation was the real thing, and when she was acquitted the world began to revolve again.

That justice had been flouted mattered nothing. Hammett, curiously, believed her innocent. Like many successful lawyers he had based his career on the principle of prosecuting the guilty and defending the innocent—this way he was sure of a sufficiently high proportion of successes to give him a reputation for being brilliant and unbeatable. When he defended Gloria Tremayne most lawyers thought he had been tempted to depart from principle by a fat bribe from her studio, but in fact he volunteered to take the case. Perhaps he, too, was working off a secret infatuation.

Of course, I never saw her again. As soon as her next picture had been safely released her studio dropped her. Later she briefly reappeared on a narcotics charge after a car smash, and then disappeared into a limbo of alcoholics hospitals and psycho wards. When she died five years afterwards few newspapers gave her more than a couple of lines.

Below, Stamers sounded the horn. Leisurely I retraced my way through the lounge and bedrooms, scanning the empty floors, running my hands over the smooth plastex walls, bracing myself to feel again the impact of Gloria Tremayne's personality. Blissfully, her presence would be everywhere in the house, a thousand echoes of her distilled into every matrix and senso-cell, each moment of emotion blended into a replica of her more intimate than anyone, apart from her dead husband, could ever know. The Gloria Tremayne with whom I had become infatuated had ceased to exist, but this house was the shrine that entombed the very signatures of her soul.

To begin with everything went quietly. Fay remonstrated with me, but I promised her a new mink wrap out of the savings we made on the house. Secondly, I was careful to keep the volume down for the first few weeks, so that there would be no clash of feminine wills—one major problem of psychotropic houses is that after several months one has to increase the volume to get the same image of the last owner, and this increases the sensitivity of the memory cells and their rate of contamination. At the same time, magnifying the psychic underlay emphasizes the cruder emotional ground-base, one begins to taste the lees rather than the distilled cream of the previous tenancy. I wanted to savor the quintessence of Gloria Tremayne as long as possible so I deliberately rationed myself, turning the volume down during the day while I was out, then switching on only those rooms in which I sat in the evenings.

Right from the outset I was neglecting Fay. Not only were we both preoccupied with the usual problems of psychic adjustment faced by every married couple moving into a new house—undressing in the master bedroom that first night was a positive honeymoon debut all over again—but I was completely immersed in the strange and exhilarating persona of Gloria Tremayne, exploring every alcove and niche in search of her.

In the evenings I sat in the library, feeling her around me in the gently stirring walls, hovering nearby as I emptied the packing cases like an attendant succubus. Sipping my Scotch while night closed in over the dark blue pool, I carefully analyzed her personality, deliberately varying my moods to evoke as wide a range of responses. The memory cells in the house were perfectly bonded, never revealing any flaws of character, always reposed and self-controlled. If I leapt out of my chair and switched the stereogram abruptly from Stravinsky to Stan Kenton to the MJQ, the room adjusted its mood and tempo without effort.

And yet how long was it before I discovered that there was another personality present in that house, and began to feel the curious eerieness Fay and I had noticed, like everyone else, as soon as Stamers switched the house on? Not for a few weeks, when the house was still responding to my starstruck idealism. While my devotion to the parted spirit of Gloria Tremayne was the dominant mood, the house played itself back accordingly, recapitulating only the more serene aspects of Gloria Tremayne's character.

Soon, however, the mirror was to darken.

It was Fay who broke the spell. She quickly realized that the initial responses were being overlayed by others from a more mellow and, from her point of view, more dangerous quarter of the past. After doing her best to put up with them she made a few guarded attempts to freeze Gloria out, switching the volume controls up and down, selecting the maximum of base lift—which stressed the masculine responses—and the minimum of alto lift.

One morning I caught her on her knees by the console, poking a screwdriver at the memory drum, apparently in an effort to erase the entire store.

Taking it from her, I locked the unit and hooked the key onto my chain.

"Darling, the mortgage company could sue us for destroying the pedigree. Without it this house would be valueless. What are you trying to do?"

Fay dusted her hands on her skirt and stared me straight in the eye, chin jutting.

"I'm trying to restore a little sanity here, Howard; if possible, find my own marriage again. I thought it might be in there somewhere."

I put my arm around her, steered her back towards the kitchen. "Darling, you're getting over-intuitive again. Just relax, don't try to upset everything."

"Upset—? Howard, what are you talking about? Haven't I a right to my own husband? I'm sick of sharing him with a homicidal neurotic who died five years ago. It's positively ghoulish!"

I winced as she snapped this out, feeling the walls in the hallway darken and retreat defensively. The air became clouded and frenetic, like a dull storm-filled day.

"Fay, you know your talent for exaggeration. . . ." I searched around for the kitchen, momentarily disoriented as the corridor walls shifted and backed. "You don't know how lucky you—"

I didn't get any further before she interrupted. Within five seconds we were in the middle of a blistering row. Fay threw all caution to the winds, deliberately, I think, in the hope of damaging the house permanently, while I stupidly let a lot of my unconscious resentment towards her come out. Finally she stormed away into her bedroom and I stamped back into the shattered lounge and slumped down angrily on the sofa.

Above me the ceiling flexed and quivered, the color of roof slates, here and there mottled by angry veins that bunched the walls in on each other. The air pressure mounted but I felt too tired to open a window and sat stewing in a pit of black anger.

It must have been then that I recognized the presence of Miles Vanden Starr. All echoes of Gloria Tremayne's personality had vanished, and for the first time since moving in I had recovered my normal perspectives. The mood of anger and resentment in the lounge was remarkably persistent, far longer than expected from what had been little more than a tiff. The walls continued to pulse and knot for over half an hour, long after my own irritation had faded and I was sitting up and examining the room clear-headedly.

The anger, deep and frustrated, was obviously masculine, and I assumed, correctly, that the original source had been Vanden Starr, who had designed the house for Gloria Tremayne and lived there for over a year before his death. To have so grooved the memory drum meant that this atmosphere of blind, neurotic hostility had been maintained for most of that time.

As the resentment slowly dispersed I could see that for the time being Fay had succeeded in her object. The serene persona of Gloria Tremayne had vanished. The feminine motif was still there, in a higher shriller key, but the dominant presence was distinctly Vanden Starr's. This new mood of the house reminded me of the courtroom photographs of him, glowering out of 1950-ish groups with Le Corbusier and Lloyd Wright, stalking about some housing project in Chicago or Tokyo like a petty dictator, heavy-jowled, thyroidal, with large lustreless eyes, and then the Vermilion Sands: 1970 shots of him, fitting into the movie colony like a shark into a gold-fish bowl.

However, he had designed some brilliant architecture, and there was power behind those baleful drives. Cued in by our tantrum, the presence of Vanden Starr had descended upon 99 Stellavista like a thundercloud. At first I tried to recapture the earlier halcyon mood, but this had disappeared and my irritation at loosing it only served to inflate the thundercloud. An unfortunate aspect of psychotropic houses is the factor of resonance—diametrically opposed personalities soon stabilize their relationship, the echo inevitably yielding to the new source. But where the personalities are of similar frequency and amplitude they mutually reinforce themselves, each adapting itself for comfort to the personality of the other. All too soon I began to assume the character of Vanden Starr, and my increased exasperation with Fay merely drew from the house a harder front of antagonism.

Later I knew that I was, in fact, treating Fay in exactly the way that Vanden Starr had treated Gloria Tremayne, recapitulating the steps of their tragedy with consequences that were equally disastrous.

Fay recognized the changed mood of the house immediately. "What's happened to our lodger?" she gibed at dinner the next evening. "Our beautiful ghost seems to be spurning you. Is the spirit unwilling although the flesh is weak?"

"God knows," I growled testily. "I think you've really messed the place up." I glanced around the dining room for any echo of Gloria Tremayne, but she had gone. Fay went out to the kitchen and I sat over my half-eaten hors d'oeuvres, staring at it blankly, when I felt a curious ripple in the wall behind me, a silver dart of movement that vanished as soon as I looked up. I tried to focus it without success, the first echo of Gloria since our row, but later that evening, when I went into Fay's bedroom after I heard her crying, I noticed it again.

Fay had gone into the bathroom. About to find her I felt the same echo of feminine anguish. It had been prompted by Fay's tears, but like Vanden Starr's mood set off by my own anger, it persisted long after the original cue. I followed it into the corridor as it faded out of the room but it diffused outwards into the ceiling and hung there motionlessly.

Starting to walk down to the lounge, I realized that the house was watching me like a wounded animal.

Two days later came the attack on Fay.

I had just returned home from the office, childishly annoyed with Fay for parking her car on my side of the garage. In the cloakroom I tried to check my anger; the senso-cells had picked up the cue and began to suck hate and irritation out of me, pouring it back into the air until the walls of the cloakroom darkened and began to seethe.

I shouted some gratuitous insult at Fay, who was in the lounge, then heard her cry out. A second later she screamed: "Howard! Quickly!"

Running towards the lounge, I flung myself at the door, expecting it to retract. Instead, it remained rigid, frame locked in the archway. The entire house seemed grey and strained, the pool outside like a tank of cold lead.

Fay shouted again. I seized the metal handle of the manual control and wrenched the door back.

Fay was almost out of sight, on one of the slab sofas in the center of the room, buried beneath the sagging canopy of the ceiling which had collapsed onto her. The heavy plastex had flowed together directly above her head, forming a blob a yard in diameter.

Raising the flaccid grey plastex with my hands, I managed to lift it off Fay, who was spread-eagled back into the cushions with only her feet protruding. She wriggled out and flung her arms around me, sobbing noiselessly.

"Howard, this house is insane, I think it's trying to kill me!"

"For heaven's sake, Fay, don't be silly. It was simply a freak accumulation of senso-cells. Your breathing probably set it off." I patted her shoulder, remembering the child I had married a few years earlier. Smiling to myself, I watched the ceiling retract slowly, the walls grow lighter in tone.

"Howard, can't we leave here?" Fay babbled. "Let's go and live in a static house. I know it's dull, but what does it matter—?"

"Well," I said, "it's not just dull, it's dead. Don't worry, angel, you'll get to like it here."

Fay twisted away from me. "Howard, I can't stay in this house any more. You've been getting so preoccupied recently, you're changing completely." She started to cry again, then pointed at the ceiling. "If I hadn't been lying down, do you realize it would have killed me?"

I nodded, then dusted the end of the sofa. "Yes, I can see your heel marks." Irritation welled up like bile before I could stop it. "I thought I told you not to stretch out here. This isn't a beach, Fay. You know it annoys me."

Around us the walls began to mottle and cloud again.

Why did Fay anger me so easily? Was it, as I assumed at the time, unconscious resentment that egged me on, or was I merely a vehicle for the antagonism which had accumulated during Vanden Starr's marriage to Gloria Tremayne and was now venting itself on the hapless couple who followed them to 99 Stellavista? Perhaps I'm over-charitable to myself in assuming the latter, but Fay and I had been tolerably happy during our five years of marriage, and I am sure my nostalgic infatuation for Gloria Tremayne couldn't have so swept me off my feet.

Either way, however, Fay didn't wait for a second attempt. Two days later I came home to find a fresh tape on the kitchen memophone, switched it on to hear her tell me that she could no longer put up with me, my nagging or 99 Stellavista and was going back east to stay with her sister.

Callously, my first reaction, after the initial twinge of indignation, was sheer relief. I still believed that Fay was responsible for Gloria Tremayne's eclipse and the emergence of Vanden Starr, and that with her gone I would recapture the early days of idyll and romance.

I was only partly right. Gloria Tremayne did return, but not in the role expected. I, who had helped to defend her at her trial, should have known better.

A few days after Fay left I became aware that the house had taken on a separate existence, its coded memories discharging themselves independently of my own behavior. Often when I returned in the evening, eager to relax over half a decanter of Scotch, I would find the ghosts of Miles Vanden Starr and Gloria Tremayne in full flight, Starr's black menacing personality crowding after the tenuous but increasingly resilient quintessence of his wife. This rapierlike resistance could be observed literally—the walls of the lounge would stiffen and darken in a vortex of dull anger that converged upon a small zone of lightness hiding in one of the alcoves, as if to obliterate its presence, but at the last moment Gloria's persona would flit nimbly away, leaving the room to seethe and writhe.

Fay had set off this spirit of resistance, and I visualized Gloria Tremayne going through a similar period of living hell. As her personality re-emerged in its new role I watched it carefully, volume at maximum despite the damage the house might do to itself. Once Stamers stopped by and offered to get the circuits checked for me. He had seen the house from the road, flexing and changing color like an anguished squid. Thanking him, I made up some excuse and declined. (Later he told me that I kicked him out unceremoniously— apparently he hardly recognized me, I was striding around the dark quaking house like a madman in an Elizabethan horror tragedy, oblivious of everything.)

Although submerged by the personality of Miles Vanden Starr, I gradually realized that Gloria Tremayne had been deliberately driven out of her mind by him. What had prompted his implacable hostility I can only hazard—perhaps he resented her success, perhaps she had been unfaithful to him. When she finally retaliated and shot him it was, I'm sure, an act of self-defense.

Two months after she went east Fay filed a divorce suit against me. Frantically I telephoned her, explaining I'd be grateful if she held off as the publicity would probably kill the new office. However, Fay was adamant. What annoyed me most was that she sounded better than she had done for years, really happy again. When I pleaded she said she needed the divorce in order to marry again, and then, as a last straw, refused to tell me who the man was.

By the time I slammed the phone down my temper was taking off like a five-stage lunar probe. I left the office early and began a tour of the bars in Red Beach, working my way slowly back to Vermilion Sands. I hit 99 Stellavista like a one-man Siegfried Line, mowing down most of the magnolias in the drive, ramming the car into the garage on the third pass after wrecking both auto-doors.

My keys jammed in the door lock and I finally had to kick my way through one of the glass panels. Raging upstairs onto the darkened terrace I flung my hat and coat into the pool and then slammed into the lounge. By 2 a.m., as I mixed myself a nightcap at the bar and put the last act of *Gotterdammerung* on the stereogram, the whole place was really warming up.

On the way to bed I lurched into Fay's room to see what damage I could do to the memories I still retained of her, kicked in a wardrobe and booted the mattress onto the floor, turning the walls literally blue with a salvo of choice epithets.

Shortly after 3 o'clock, the decanter spilt onto the bed, I fell asleep in my room, the house revolving around me like an enormous turntable.

It must have been only 4 o'clock when I woke, conscious of a curious silence in the darkened room. I was stretched across the bed, one hand around the neck of the decanter, the other holding a dead cigar stub. The walls were motionless, unstirred by even the residual eddies which drift through a psychotropic house when the occupants are asleep.

Something had altered the normal perspectives of the room. Trying to focus on the grey underswell of the ceiling, I listened for footsteps outside. Sure enough, the corridor wall began to retract slightly, the archway, usually a six-inch wide slit, rising to admit someone. Nothing came through, but the room expanded to accommodate an additional presence, the ceiling ballooning upwards. Astounded, I tried not to move my head, watching the unoccupied pressure zone move quickly across the room towards the bed, its motion shadowed by a small dome in the ceiling.

The pressure zone paused at the foot of the bed and hesitated for a few seconds. But instead of stabilizing, the walls began to vibrate rapidly, quivering with strange uncertain tremors, radiating a sensation of acute urgency and indecision.

Then, abruptly, the room stilled. A second later, as I lifted myself up on one elbow, a violent spasm convulsed the room, buckling the walls and lifting the bed off the floor. The entire house started to shake and writhe. Gripped by this seizure, the bedroom contracted and expanded like the chamber of a dying heart, the ceiling rising and falling, floor yawing.

I steadied myself on the swinging bed and gradually the convulsion died away, the walls realigning. I stood up, wondering what insane crisis this psychotropic *grande mal* duplicated, and bumped my head sharply on the ceiling.

The room was in darkness, thin moonlight coming through the trio of small circular vents behind the bed. These were contracting as the walls closed in on each other. Pressing my hands against the ceiling, I felt it push downwards strongly. The edges of the floor were blending into the walls as the room converted itself into a sphere.

The air pressure mounted. I stumbled over to the vents, reached them as they clamped around my fists, air whistling out through my fingers. Face against the openings, I gulped in the cool night air, then tried to force apart the locking plastex.

The safety cut-out switch was above the door on the other side of the room. I dived across to it, clambering over the tilting bed, but the flowing plastex had submerged the whole unit.

Head bent to avoid the ceiling, I pulled off my tie, gasping at the thudding air. Trapped in the room, I was suffocating as it duplicated the expiring breaths of Vanden Starr after he had been shot. The tremendous spasm had been his convulsive reaction as the bullet from Gloria Tremayne's gun had crashed into his chest.

I fumbled in my pockets for a knife, felt my cigarette lighter, then pulled it out and flicked it on. The room was now a grey sphere ten feet in diameter, thick veins, as broad as my arm, knotting across its surface, crushing the endboards of the bedstead.

Brain pounding, I raised the lighter to the surface of the ceiling, let it play across the opaque fluoglass. Immediately it began to fizz and bubble, suddenly flared alight and split apart, the two burning lips unzipping in a brilliant discharge of heat.

As the cocoon bisected itself, I could see the twisted mouth of the corridor bending down into the room, below the sagging outline of the dining room ceiling. Feet skating in the molten plastex, I pulled myself up onto the corridor. The whole house seemed to have been ruptured. Walls were buckled, floors furling at their edges, water pouring out of the pool as the unit tipped forwards on the weakened foundations. The glass slabs of the staircase had been shattered, the razor-like teeth jutting out of the wall.

I ran into Fay's bedroom, found the cut-out switch and stabbed the sprinkler alarm.

The house was still throbbing slightly, but a moment later it locked and became rigid. I leaned against the dented wall and let the spray pour across my face from the sprinkler jets.

Around me, its wings torn and disarrayed, the house reared up like a tortured flower.

Standing in the middle of one of the trampled flower beds, Stamers gazed up at the house, an expression of awe and bewilderment on his face. It was just after 6 o'clock and the last of the three police cars had driven off, the lieutenant in charge finally conceding defeat. "Dammit, I can't arrest a house for attempted homicide, can I?" he'd asked me somewhat belligerently. I roared with laughter at this, my initial feelings of shock having given way to an almost hysterical sense of fun.

Stamers found me equally difficult to understand.

"What on earth were you doing in there?" he asked, voice down to a whisper.

"Nothing. I tell you I was fast asleep. And relax. The house can't hear you. It's switched off."

We wandered across the churned gravel and waded through the water which lay like a huge black mirror across the front half of the lawn. Stamers shook his head. The house looked like a surrealist nightmare, all the perspectives a slipped, angles displaced.

"The place must have been insane," Stamers murmured. "If you ask me if needs a psychiatrist to straighten it out."

"You're right there," I told him. "In fact, that was exactly my role—to reconstruct the original traumatic situation in order to release the repressed material."

"Why joke about it? It tried to kill you."

"Don't be absurd. The real culprit is Vanden Starr, but as the lieutenant implied, you can't arrest a man who's been dead for ten years. It was the pent-up memory of his death which finally erupted from the house's memory and tried to kill me. Even if Gloria Tremayne was driven into pulling the trigger, Starr pointed the gun. Believe me, I lived out his role for a couple of months. What worries me is that if Fay hadn't had enough good sense to leave me she might have been hypnotized by the persona of Gloria Tremayne into killing *me*, and probably would have died for it."

Much to Stamers' surprise, I decided to stay on at 99 Stellavista. Apart from the fact that I hadn't enough cash to buy another place, the house had certain undeniable memories for me that I didn't want to forsake. Gloria Tremayne was still there, and I was sure that Vanden Starr had at last gone. The kitchen and service units were still functional, and apart from the weird contorted shapes most of the rooms were habitable.

In addition I needed a rest, and there's nothing so quiet as a static house.

Of course, in its present form 99 Stellavista can hardly be regarded as a typical static dwelling. Yet, the deformed rooms and twisted corridors have as much personality as any psychotropic house.

The PT unit is still working and one day I shall switch it on again. But one thing worries me. The violent spasms which ruptured the house may in some way have damaged Gloria Tremayne's personality, and the tortured walls and ceilings reflect the twisted partitions of her now warped mind. To live with it might well be madness for me, as there's a subtle captivating charm about the house even in its distorted form, like the ambiguous smile of a beautiful but insane woman.

Often I unlock the control console and examine the memory drum. Her personality, whatever it may be, is there. Nothing would be simpler than to erase it. But I can't.

One day soon, whatever the outcome, I know that I shall have to switch the house on again.

THE CAGE OF SAND

At sunset, when the vermilion glow reflected from the dunes along the horizon fitfully illuminated the white faces of the abandoned hotels, Bridgman stepped on to his balcony and looked out over the long stretches of cooling sand as the tides of purple shadow seeped across them. Slowly, extending their slender fingers through the shallow saddles and depressions, the shadows massed together like gigantic combs, a few phosphorescing spurs of obsidian isolated for a moment between the tines, and then finally coalesced and flooded in a solid wave across the half-submerged hotels. Behind the silent facades, in the tilting sand-filled streets which had once glittered with cocktail bars and restaurants, it was already night. Haloes of moonlight beaded the lamp-standards with silver dew, and draped the shuttered windows and slipping cornices like a frost of frozen gas.

As Bridgman watched, his lean bronzed arms propped against the rusting rail, the last whorls of light sank away into the cerise funnel withdrawing below the horizon, and the first wind stirred across the dead Martian sand. Here and there miniature cyclones whirled about a sand-spur, drawing off swirling feathers of moon-washed spray, and a nimbus of white dust swept across the dunes and settled in the dips and hollows. Gradually the drifts accumulated, edging towards the former shoreline below the hotels. Already the first four floors had been inundated, and the sand now reached up to within two feet of Bridgman's balcony. After the next sand-storm he would be forced yet again to move to the floor above.

"Bridgman!"

The voice cleft the darkness like a spear. Fifty yards to his right, at the edge of the derelict sand-break he had once attempted to build below the hotel, a square stocky figure wearing a pair of frayed cotton shorts waved up at him. The moonlight etched the broad sinewy muscles of his chest, the powerful bowed legs sinking almost to their calves in the soft Martian sand. He was about forty-five years old, his thinning hair close-cropped so that he seemed almost bald. In his right hand he carried a large canvas hold-all.

Bridgman smiled to himself. Standing there patiently in the moonlight below the derelict hotel, Travis reminded him of some long-delayed tourist arriving at a ghost resort years after its extinction.

"Bridgman, are you coming?" When the latter still leaned on his balcony rail, Travis added: "The next conjunction is tomorrow."

Bridgman shook his head, a rictus of annoyance twisting his mouth. He hated the bi-monthly conjunctions, when all seven of the derelict satellite capsules still orbiting the Earth crossed the sky together. Invariably on these nights he remained in his room, playing over the old memo-tapes he had salvaged from the submerged chalets and motels further along the beach (the hysterical "This is Mamie Goldberg, 62955 Cocoa Boulevard, I really wanna protest against this crazy evacuation . . ." or resigned "Sam Snade here, the Pontiac convertible in the back garage belongs to anyone who can dig it out.") Travis and Louise Woodward always came to the hotel on the conjunction nights—it was the highest building in the resort, with an unrestricted view from horizon to horizon—and would follow the seven converging stars as they pursued their endless courses around the globe. Both would be oblivious of everything else, which the wardens knew only too well, and they reserved their most careful searches of the sand-sea for these bi-monthly occasions. Invariably Bridgman found himself forced to act as look-out for the other two.

"I was out last night," he called down to Travis. "Keep away from the north-east perimeter fence by the Cape. They'll be busy repairing the track."

Most nights Bridgman divided his time between excavating the buried motels for caches of supplies (the former inhabitants of the resort area had assumed the government would soon rescind its evacuation order) and disconnecting the sections of metal roadway laid across the desert for the wardens' jeeps. Each of the squares of wire mesh was about five yards wide and weighed over three hundred pounds. After he had snapped the lines of rivets, dragged the sections away and buried them among the dunes he would be exhausted, and spend most of the next day nursing his strained hands and shoulders. Some sections of the track were now permanently anchored with heavy steel stakes, and he knew that sooner or later they would be unable to delay the wardens by sabotaging the roadway.

Travis hesitated, and with a noncommittal shrug disappeared among the dunes, the heavy tool-bag swinging easily from one powerful arm. Despite the meagre diet which sustained him, his energy and determination seemed undiminished—in a single night Brigman had watched him dismantle twenty sections of track and then loop together the adjacent limbs of a cross-road, sending an entire convoy of six vehicles off into the waste-lands to the south.

Bridgman turned from the balcony, then stopped when a faint tang of brine touched the cool air. Ten miles away, hidden by the lines of dunes, was the sea, the long green rollers of the middle Atlantic breaking against the red Martian strand. When he had first come to the beach five years earlier there had never been the faintest scent of brine across the intervening miles of sand. Slowly, however, the Atlantic was driving the shore back to its former margins. The tireless shoulder of the Gulf Stream drummed against the soft Martian dust and piled the dunes into grotesque rococo reefs which the wind carried away into the sand-sea. Gradually the ocean was returning, reclaiming its great smooth basin, sifting out the black quartz and Martian obsidian which would never be wind-borne and drawing these down into its deeps. More and more often the stain of brine would hang on the evening air, reminding Bridgman why he had first come to the beach and removing any inclination to leave.

Three years earlier he had attempted to measure the rate of approach, by driving a series of stakes into the sand at the water's edge, but the shifting contours of the dunes carried away the coloured poles. Later, using the promontory at Cape Canaveral, where the old launching gantries and landing ramps reared up into the sky like derelict pieces of giant sculpture, he had calculated by triangulation that the advance was little more than thirty yards per year. At this rate—without wanting to, he had automatically made the calculation—it would be well over five hundred years before the Atlantic reached its former littoral at Cocoa Beach. Though discouragingly slow, the movement was nonetheless in a forward direction, and Bridgman was happy to remain in his hotel ten miles away across the dunes, conceding towards its time of arrival the few years he had at his disposal.

Later, shortly after Louise Woodward's arrival, he had thought of dismantling one of the motel cabins and building himself a small chalet by the water's edge. But the shoreline had been too dismal and forbidding. The great red dunes rolled on for miles, cutting off half the sky, dissolving slowly under the impact of the slate-green water. There was no formal tide-line, but only a steep shelf littered with nodes of quartz and rusting fragments of Mars rockets brought back with the ballast. He spent a few days in a cave below a towering sand-reef, watching the long galleries of compacted red dust crumble and dissolve as the cold Atlantic stream sluiced through them, collapsing like the decorated colonnades of a baroque cathedral. In the summer the heat reverberated from the hot sand as from the slag of some molten sun, burning the rubber soles from his boots, and the light from the scattered flints of washed quartz flickered with diamond hardness. Bridgman had returned to the hotel grateful for his room overlooking the silent dunes.

Leaving the balcony, the sweet smell of brine still in his nostrils, he went over to the desk. A small cone of shielded light shone down over the tape recorder and rack of spools. The rumble of the wardens' unsilenced engines always gave him at least five minutes' warning of their arrival, and it would have been safe to install another lamp in the room—there were no roadways between the hotel and the sea, and from a distance any light reflected on to the balcony was indistinguishable from the corona of glimmering phosphors which hung over the sand like myriads of fire-flies. However, Bridgman preferred to sit in the darkened suite, enclosed by the circle of books on the makeshift shelves, the shadow-filled air playing over his shoulders through the long night as he toyed with the memo-tapes, fragments of a vanished and unregretted past. By day he always drew the blinds, immolating himself in a world of perpetual twilight.

Bridgman had easily adapted himself to his self-isolation, soon evolved a system of daily routines that gave him the maximum of time to spend on his private reveries. Pinned to the walls around him were a series of huge white-prints and architectural drawings, depicting various elevations of a fantastic Martian city he had once designed, its glass spires and curtain walls rising like heliotropic jewels from the vermilion desert. In fact, the whole city was a vast piece of jewellery, each elevation brilliantly visualised but as symmetrical, and ultimately as lifeless, as a crown. Bridgman continuously retouched the drawings, inserting more and more details, so that they almost seemed to be photographs of an original.

Most of the hotels in the town—one of a dozen similar resorts buried by the sand which had once formed an unbroken strip of motels, chalets and five-star hotels thirty miles to the south of Cape Canaveral—were well stocked with supplies of canned food abandoned when the area was evacuated and wired off. There were ample reservoirs and cisterns filled with water, apart from a thousand intact cocktail bars six feet below the surface of the sand. Travis had excavated a dozen of these in search of his favourite vintage bourbon. Walking out across the desert behind the town one would suddenly find a short flight of steps cut into the annealed sand and crawl below an occluded sign announcing 'The Satellite Bar' or 'The Orbit Room' into the inner sanctum, where the jetting deck of a chromium bar had been cleared as far as the diamond-paned mirror freighted with its rows of bottles and figurines. Bridgman would have been glad to see them left undisturbed.

The whole trash of amusement arcades and cheap bars on the outskirts of the beach resorts were a depressing commentary on the original space-flights, reducing them to the level of monster side-shows at a carnival.

Outside his room, steps sounded along the corridor, then slowly climbed the stairway, pausing for a few seconds at every landing. Bridgman lowered the memo-tape in his hand, listening to the familiar tired footsteps. This was Louise Woodward, making her invariable evening ascent to the roof ten storeys above. Bridgman glanced to the timetable pinned to the wall. Only two of the satellites would be visible, between 12-25 and 12-35 a.m., at an elevation of

62 degrees in the south-west, passing through Cetus and Eridanus, neither of them containing her husband. Although the siting was two hours away, she was already taking up her position, and would remain there until dawn.

Bridgman listened wanly to the feet recede slowly up the stair-well. All through the night the slim pale-faced woman would sit out under the moon-lit sky, as the soft Martian sand her husband had given his life to reach sifted around her in the dark wind, stroking her faded hair like some mourning mariner's wife waiting for the sea to surrender her husband's body. Travis usually joined her later, and the two of them sat side by side against the elevator house, the frosted letters of the hotel's neon sign strewn around their feet like the fragments of a dismembered zodiac, then at dawn made their way down into the shadow-filled streets to their eyries in the nearby hotels.

Initially Bridgman often joined their nocturnal vigil, but after a few nights he began to feel something repellent, if not actually ghoulish, about their mindless contemplation of the stars. This was not so much because of the macabre spectacle of the dead astronauts orbiting the planet in their capsules, but because of the curious sense of unspoken communion between Travis and Louise Woodward, almost as if they were celebrating a private rite to which Bridgman could never be initiated. Whatever their original motives, Bridgman sometimes suspected that these had been overlayed by other, more personal ones.

Ostensibly, Louise Woodward was watching her husband's satellite in order to keep alive his memory, but Bridgman guessed that the memories she unconsciously wished to perpetuate were those of herself twenty years earlier, when her husband had been a celebrity and she herself courted by magazine columnists and TV reporters. For fifteen years after his death—Woodward had been killed testing a new lightweight launching platform—she had lived a nomadic existence, driving restlessly in her cheap car from motel to motel across the continent, following her husband's star as it disappeared into the eastern night, and had at last made her home at Cocoa Beach in sight of the rusting gantries across the bay.

Travis's real motives were probably more complex. To Bridgman, after they had known each other for a couple of years, he had confided that he felt himself bound by a debt of honour to maintain a watch over the dead astronauts for the example of courage and sacrifice they had set him as a child (although most of them had been piloting their wrecked capsules for fifty years before Travis's birth), and that now they were virtually forgotten he must single-handedly keep alive the fading flame of their memory. Bridgman was convinced of his sincerity.

Yet later, going through a pile of old news magazines in the trunk of a car he excavated from a motel port, he came across a picture of Travis wearing an aluminium pressure suit and learned something more of his story. Apparently Travis had at one time been himself an astronaut—or rather, a would-be astronaut. A test pilot for one of the civilian agencies setting up orbital relay stations, his nerve had failed him a few seconds before the last 'hold' of his count-down, a moment of pure unexpected funk that cost the company some five million dollars.

Obviously it was his inability to come to terms with this failure of character, unfortunately discovered lying flat on his back on a contour couch two hundred feet above the launching pad, which had brought Travis to Canaveral, the abandoned Mecca of the first heroes of astronautics.

Tactfully Bridgman had tried to explain that no-one would blame him for this failure of nerve—less his responsibility than that of the selectors who had picked him for the flight, or at least the result of an unhappy concatenation of ambiguously worded multiple-choice questions (crosses in the wrong boxes, some heavier to bear and harder to open than others! Bridgman had joked sardonically to himself). But Travis seemed to have reached his own decision about himself. Night after night, he watched the brilliant funerary convoy weave its gilded pathway towards the dawn sun, salving his own failure by identifying it with the greater, but blameless, failure of the seven astronauts. Travis still wore his hair in the regulation 'mohican' cut of the space-man, still kept himself in perfect physical trim by the vigorous routines he had practised before his abortive flight. Sustained by the personal myth he had created, he was now more or less unreachable.

"Dear Harry, I've taken the car and deposit box. Sorry it should end like—"

Irritably, Bridgman switched off the memo-tape and its recapitulation of some thirty-year-old private triviality. For some reason he seemed unable to accept Travis and Louise Woodward for what they were. He disliked this failure of compassion, a nagging compulsion to expose other people's motives and strip away the insulating sheaths around their naked nerve strings, particularly as his own motives for being at Cape Canaveral were so suspect. Why was *he* there, what failure was *he* trying to expiate? And why choose Cocoa Beach as his penitential shore? For three years he had asked himself these questions so often that they had ceased to have any meaning, like a fossilised catechism or the blunted self-recrimination of a paranoic.

He had resigned his job as the chief architect of a big space development company after the large government contract on which the firm depended, for the design of the first Martian city-settlement, was awarded to a rival consortium. Secretly, however, he realised that his resignation had marked his unconscious acceptance that despite his great imaginative gifts he was unequal to the specialised and more prosaic tasks of designing the settlement. On the drawing board, as elsewhere, he would always remain earth-bound.

His dreams of building a new gothic architecture of launching ports and controls gantries, of being the Frank Lloyd Wright and Le Corbusier of the first city to be raised outside Earth, faded forever, but leaving him unable to accept the alternative of turning out endless plans for low-cost hospitals in Ecuador and housing estates in Tokyo. For a year he had drifted aimlessly, but a few colour photographs of the vermilion sunsets at Cocoa Beach and a news story about the recluses living on in the submerged motels had provided a powerful compass.

He dropped the memo-tape into a drawer, making an effort to accept Louise Woodward and Travis on their own terms, a wife keeping watch over her dead husband and an old astronaut maintaining a solitary vigil over the memories of his lost comrades-in-arms.

The wind gusted against the balcony window, and a light spray of sand rained across the floor. At night dust-storms churned along the beach. Thermal pools isolated by the cooling desert would suddenly accrete like beads of quicksilver and erupt across the fluffy sand in miniature tornadoes.

Only fifty yards away, the dying cough of a heavy diesel cut through the shadows. Quickly Bridgman turned off the small desk light, grateful for his meanness over the battery packs plugged into the circuit, then stepped to the window. At the leftward edge of the sand-break, half-hidden in the long shadows cast by the hotel, was a large tracked vehicle with a low camouflaged hull. A narrow observation bridge had been built over the bumpers directly in front of the squat snout of the engine housing, and two of the beach wardens were craning up through the plexiglass windows at the balconies of the hotel, shifting their binoculars from room to room. Behind them, under the glass dome of the extended driving cabin, were three more wardens, controlling an out-board spot-light. In the centre of the bowl a thin mote of light pulsed with the rhythm of the engine, ready to throw its powerful beam into any of the open rooms.

Bridgman hid back behind the shutters as the binoculars focussed upon the adjacent balcony, moved to his own, hesitated, and passed to the next. Exasperated by the sabotaging of the roadways, the wardens had evidently decided on a new type of vehicle. Wtih their four broad tracks, the huge squat sand-cars would be free of the mesh roadways and able to rove at will through the dunes and sand-hills.

Bridgman watched the vehicle reverse slowly, its engine barely varying its deep base growl, then move off along the line of hotels, almost indistinguishable in profile among the shifting dunes and hillocks. A hundred yards away, at the first intersection, it turned towards the main boulevard, wisps of dust streaming from the metal cleats like thin spumes of steam. The men in the observation bridge were still watching the hotel. Bridgman was certain that they had seen a reflected glimmer of light, or perhaps some movement of Louise Woodward's on the roof. However reluctant to leave the car and be contaminated by the poisonous dust, the wardens would not hesitate if the capture of one of the beachcombers warranted it.

Racing up the staircase, Bridgman made his way to the roof, crouching below the windows that overlooked the boulevard. Like a huge crab, the sand-car had parked under the jutting overhang of the big department store opposite. Once fifty feet from the ground, the concrete lip was now separated from it by little more than six or seven feet, and the sand-car was hidden in the shadows below it, engine silent. A single movement in a window, or the unexpected return of Travis, and the wardens would spring from the hatchways, their long-handled nets and lassoes pinioning them around the necks and ankles. Bridgman remembered one beachcomber he had seen flushed from his motel hideout and carried off like a huge twitching spider at the centre of a black rubber web, the wardens with their averted faces and masked mouths like devils in an abstract ballet.

Reaching the roof, Bridgman stepped out into the opaque white moonlight. Louise Woodward was leaning on the balcony, looking out towards the distant, unseen sea. At the faint sound of the door creaking she turned and began to walk listlessly around the roof, her pale face floating like a nimbus. She wore a freshly ironed print dress she had found in a rusty spin drier in one of the launderettes, and her streaked blonde hair floated out lightly behind her on the wind.

"Louise!"

Involuntarily she started, tripping over a fragment of the neon sign, then moved backwards towards the balcony overlooking the boulevard.

"Mrs. Woodward!" Bridgman held her by the elbow, raised a hand to her mouth before she could cry out. "The wardens are down below. They're watching the hotel. We must find Travis before he returns."

Louise hesitated, apparently recognising Bridgman only by an effort, and her eyes turned up to the black marble sky. Bridgman looked at his watch; it was almost 12-35. He searched the stars in the south-west.

Louise murmured: "They're nearly here now, I must see them. Where is Travis, he should be here?"

Bridgman pulled at her arm. "Perhaps he saw the sand-car. Mrs. Woodward, we should leave."

Suddenly she pointed up at the sky, then wrenched away from him and ran to the rail. "There they are!"

Fretting, Bridgman waited until she had filled her eyes with the two companion points of light speeding from the western horizon. These were Merril and Pokrovski—like every schoolboy he knew the sequences perfectly, a second system of constellations with a more complex but far more tangible periodicity and precession—the Castor and Pollux of the orbiting zodiac, whose appearance always heralded a full conjunction the following night.

Louise Woodward gazed up at them from the rail, the rising wind lifting her hair off her shoulders and entraining it horizontally behind her head. Around her feet the red Martian dust swirled and rustled, silting over the fragments of the old neon sign, a brilliant pink spume streaming from her long fingers as they moved along the balcony ledge. When the satellites finally disappeared among the stars along the horizon, she leaned forwards, her face raised to the milk-blue moon as if to delay their departure, then turned back to Bridgman, a bright smile on her face.

His earlier suspicions vanishing, Bridgman smiled back at her encouragingly. "Roger will be here tomorrow night, Louise. We must be careful the wardens don't catch us before we see him."

He felt a sudden admiration for her, at the stoical way she had sustained herself during her long vigil. Perhaps she thought of Woodward as still alive, and in some way was patiently waiting for him to return? He remembered her saying once: 'Roger was only a boy when he took off, you know, I feel more like his mother now,' as if frightened how Woodward would react to her dry skin and fading hair, fearing that he might even have forgotten her. No doubt the death she visualised for him was of a different order than the mortal kind.

Hand in hand, they tiptoed carefully down the flaking steps, jumped down from a terrace window into the soft sand below the wind-break. Bridgman sank to his knees in the fine silver moon-dust, then waded up to the firmer ground, pulling Louise after him. They climbed through a breach in the tilting palisades, then ran away from the line of dead hotels looming like skulls in the empty night.

"Paul, wait!" Her head still raised to the sky, Louise Woodward fell to her knees in a hollow between two dunes, with a laugh stumbled after Bridgman as he raced through the dips and saddles. The wind was now whipping the sand off the higher crests, flurries of dust spurting like excited wavelets. A hundred yards away, the town was a fading film set, projected by the camera obscura of the sinking moon. They were standing where the long Atlantic seas had once been ten fathoms deep, and Bridgman could scent again the tang of brine among the flickering white-caps of dust, phosphorescing like shoals of animalcula. He waited for any sign of Travis.

"Louise, we'll have to go back to the town. The sand-storms are blowing up, we'll never see Travis here."

They moved back through the dunes, then worked their way among the narrow alleyways between the hotels to the northern gateway to the town. Bridgman found a vantage point in a small apartment block, and they lay down looking out below a window lintel into the sloping street, the warm sand forming a pleasant cushion. At the intersections the dust blew across the roadway in white clouds, obscuring the warden's beach-car parked a hundred yards down the boulevard.

Half an hour later an engine surged, and Bridgman began to pile sand into the interval in front of them. "They're going. Thank God!"

Louise Woodward held his arm. "Look!"

Fifty feet away, his white vinyl suit half-hidden in the dust clouds, one of the wardens was advancing slowly towards them, his lasso twirling lightly in his hand. A few feet behind was a second warden, craning up at the windows of the apartment block with his binoculars.

Bridgman and Louise crawled back below the ceiling, then dug their way under a transom into the kitchen at the rear. A window opened on to a sand-filled yard, and they darted away through the lifting dust that whirled between the buildings.

Suddenly, around a corner, they saw the line of wardens moving down a side-street, the sand-car edging along behind them. Before Bridgman could steady himself a spasm of pain seized his right calf, contorting the gastrocnemius muscle, and he fell to one knee. Louise Woodward pulled him back against the wall, then pointed at a squat, bow-legged figure trudging towards them along the curving road into town.

"Travis—"

The tool-bag swung from his right hand, and his feet rang faintly on the wire-mesh roadway. Head down, he seemed unaware of the wardens hidden by a bend in the road.

"Come on!" Disregarding the negligible margin of safety, Bridgman clambered to his feet and impetuously ran out into the centre of the street. Louise tried to stop him, and they had covered only ten yards before the wardens saw them. There was a warning shout, and the spot-light flung its giant cone down the street. The sand-car surged forward, like a massive dust-covered bull, its tracks clawing at the sand.

"Travis!" As Bridgman reached the bend, Louise Woodward ten yards behind, Travis looked up from his reverie, then flung the tool-bag over one shoulder and raced ahead of them towards the clutter of motel roofs protruding from the other side of the street. Lagging behind the others, Bridgman again felt the cramp attack his leg, broke off into a painful shuffle. When Travis came back for him Bridgman tried to wave him away, but Travis pinioned his elbow and propelled him forward like an attendant straight-arming a patient.

The dust swirling around them, they disappeared through the fading streets and out into the desert, the shouts of the beach-wardens lost in the roar and clamour of the baying engine. Around them, like the strange metallic flora of some extra-terrestrial garden, the old neon signs jutted from the red Martian sand—'Satellite Motel,' 'Planet Bar,' 'Mercury Motel.' Hiding behind them, they reached the scrub-covered dunes on the edge of the town, then picked up one of the trails that led away among the sand-reefs. There, in the deep grottos of compacted sand which hung like inverted palaces, they waited until the storm subsided. Shortly before dawn the wardens abandoned their search, unable to bring the heavy sand-car on to the disintegrating reef.

Contemptuous of the wardens, Travis lit a small fire with his cigarette lighter, burning splinters of driftwood that had gathered in the gullies. Bridgman crouched beside it, warming his hands.

"This is the first time they've been prepared to leave the sand-car," he remarked to Travis. "It means they're under orders to catch us."

Travis shrugged. "Maybe. They're extending the fence along the beach. They probably intend to seal us in forever."

"What?" Bridgman stood up with a sudden feeling of uneasiness. "Why should they? Are you sure? I mean, what would be the point?"

Travis looked up at him, a flicker of dry amusement on his bleached face. Wisps of smoke wreathed his head, curled up past the serpentine columns of the grotto to the winding interval of sky a hundred feet above. "Bridgman, forgive me saying so, but if you want to leave here, you should leave now. In a month's time you won't be able to."

Bridgman ignored this, and searched the cleft of dark sky overhead, which framed the constellation Scorpio, as if hoping to see a reflection of the distant sea. "They must be crazy. How much of this fence did you see?"

"About eight hundred yards. It won't take them long to complete. The sections are prefabricated, about forty feet high." He smiled ironically at Bridgman's discomfort. "Relax, Bridgman. If you do want to get out, you'll always be able to tunnel underneath it."

"I don't want to get out," Bridgman said coldly. "Damn them, Travis, they're turning the place into a zoo. You know it won't be the same with a fence all the way around it."

"A corner of Earth that is forever Mars." Under the high forehead, Travis's eyes were sharp and watchful. "I see their point. There hasn't been a fatal casualty now——" he glanced at Louise Woodward, who was strolling about in the colonnades "——for nearly twenty years, and passenger rockets are supposed to be as safe as commuters' trains. They're quietly sealing off the past, Louise and I and you with it. I suppose it's pretty considerate of them not to burn the place down with flame throwers. The virus would be a sufficient excuse. After all, we three are probably the only reservoirs left on the planet." He picked up a handful of red dust and examined the fine crystals with a sombre eye. "Well, Bridgman, what are you going to do?"

His thoughts discharging themselves through his mind like frantic signal flares, Bridgman walked away without answering.

Behind them, Louise Woodward wandered among the deep galleries of the grotto, crooning to herself in a low voice to the sighing rhythms of the whirling sand.

The next morning they returned to the town, wading through the deep drifts of sand that lay like a fresh fall of red snow between the hotels and stores, coruscating in the brilliant sunlight. Travis and Louise Woodward made their way towards their quarters in the motels further down the beach. Bridgman searched the still, crystal air for any signs of the wardens, but the sand-car had gone, its tracks obliterated by the storm.

In his room he found their calling card.

A huge tide of dust had flowed through the french windows and submerged the desk and bed, three feet deep against the rear wall. Outside the sand-break had been inundated, and the contours of the desert had completely altered, a few spires of obsidian marking its former perspectives like bouys on a shifting sea. Bridgman spent the morning digging out his books and equipment, dismantled the electrical system and its batteries and carried everything to the room above. He would have moved to the penthouse on the top floor, but his lights would have been visible for miles.

Settling into his new quarters, he switched on the tape recorder, heard a short clipped message in the brisk voice which had shouted orders at the wardens the previous evening. "Bridgman, this is Major Webster, deputy commandant of Cocoa Beach Reservation. On the instructions of the Anti-Viral Sub-committee of the UN General Assembly we are now building a continuous fence around the beach area. On completion no further egress will be allowed, and anyone escaping will be immediately returned to the reservation. Give yourself up now, Bridgman, before—"

Bridgman stopped the tape, then reversed the spool and erased the message, staring angrily at the instrument. Unable to settle down to the task of re-wiring the room's circuits, he paced about, fiddling with the architectural drawings propped against the wall. He felt restless and hyper-excited, perhaps because he had been trying to repress, not very successfully, precisely those doubts of which Webster had now reminded him.

He stepped on to the balcony and looked out over the desert, at the red dunes rolling to the windows directly below. For the fourth time he had moved up a floor, and the sequence of identical rooms he had occupied were like displaced images of himself seen through a prism. Their common focus, that elusive final definition of himself which he had sought for so long, still remained to be found. Timelessly the sand swept towards him, its shifting contours, approximating more closely than any other landscape he had found to complete psychic zero, enveloping his past failures and uncertainties, masking them in its enigmatic canopy.

Bridgman watched the red sand flicker and fluoresce in the steepening sunlight. He would never see Mars now, and redress the implicit failure of talent, but a workable replica of the planet was contained within the beach area.

Several million tons of the Martian top-soil had been ferried in as ballast some fifty years earlier, when it was feared that the continuous firing of planetary probes and space vehicles, and the transportation of bulk stores and equipment to Mars would fractionally lower the gravitational mass of the Earth and bring it into a tighter orbit around the Sun. Although the distance involved would be little more than a few millimetres, and barely raise the temperature of the atmosphere, its cumulative effects over an extended period might have resulted in a loss into space of the tenuous layers of the outer atmosphere, and of the radiological veil which alone made the biosphere habitable.

Over a twenty-year period a fleet of large freighters had shuttled to and from Mars, dumping the ballast into the sea near the landing grounds of Cape Canaveral. Simultaneously the Russians were filling in a small section of the Caspian Sea. The intention had been that the ballast should be swallowed by the Atlantic and Caspian waters, but all too soon it was found that the microbiological analysis of the sand had been inadequate.

At the Martian polar caps, where the original water vapour in the atmosphere had condensed, a residue of ancient organic matter formed the top-soil, a fine sandy loess containing the fossilised spores of the giant lichens and mosses which had been the last living organisms on the planet millions of years earlier. Embedded in these spores were the crystal lattices of the viruses which had once preyed on the plants, and traces of these were carried back to Earth with the Canaveral and Caspian ballast.

A few years afterwards a drastic increase in a wide range of plant diseases was noticed in the southern states of America and in the Kazakhstan and Turkmenistan republics of the Soviet Union. All over Florida there were outbreaks of blight and mosaic disease, orange plantations withered and died, stunted palms split by the roadside like dried banana skins, manila grass stiffened into paper spears in the summer heat. Within a few years the entire peninsula was transformed into a desert. The swampy jungles of the Everglades became bleached and dry, the rivers cracked husks strewn with the gleaming skeletons of crocodiles and birds, the forests petrified.

The former launching ground at Canaveral was closed, and shortly afterwards the Cocoa Beach resorts were sealed off and evacuated, billions of dollars of real estate were abandoned to the virus. Fortunately never virulent to animal hosts, its influence was confined to within a small radius of the original loess which had borne it, unless ingested by the human organism, when it symbioted with the bacteria in the gut flora, benign and unknown to the host, but devastating to vegetation thousands of miles from Canaveral if returned to the soil.

Unable to rest despite his sleepless night, Bridgman played irritably with the tape recorder. During their close escape from the wardens he had more than half-hoped they would catch him. The mysterious leg cramp was obviously psychogenic. Although unable to accept consciously the logic of Webster's argument, he would willingly have conceded to the fait accompli of physical capture, gratefully submitted to a year's quarantine at the Parasitological Cleansing Unit at Tampa, and then returned to his career as an architect, chastened but accepting his failure.

As yet, however, the opportunity for surrender had failed to offer itself. Travis appeared to be aware of his ambivalent motives; Bridgman noticed that he and Louise Woodward had made no arrangements to meet him that evening for the conjunction.

In the early afternoon he went down into the streets, ploughed through the drifts of red sand, following the footprints of Travis and Louise as they wound in and out of the side-streets, finally saw them disappear into the coarser, flint-like dunes among the submerged motels to the south of the town. Giving up, he returned through the empty, shadowless streets, now and then shouted up into the hot air, listening to the echoes boom away among the dunes.

Later that afternoon he walked out towards the north-east, picking his way carefully through the dips and hollows, crouching in the pools of shadow whenever the distant sounds of the construction gangs along the perimeter were carried across to him by the wind. Around him, in the great dust basins, the grains of red sand glittered like diamonds. Barbs of rusting metal protruded from the slopes, remnants of Mars satellites and launching stages which had fallen on to the Martian deserts and then been carried back again to Earth. One fragment which he passed, a complete section of hull plate like a concave shield, still carried part of an identification numeral, and stood upright in the dissolving sand like a door into nowhere.

Just before dusk he reached a tall spur of obsidian that reared up into the tinted cerise sky like the spire of a ruined church, climbed up among its jutting cornices and looked out across the intervening two or three miles of dunes to the perimeter. Illuminated by the last light, the metal grilles shone with a roseate glow like fairy portcullises on the edge of an enchanted sea. At least half a mile of the fence had been completed, and as he watched another of the giant prefabricated sections was cantilevered into the air and staked to the ground. Already the eastern horizon was cut off by the encroaching fence, the enclosed Martian sand like the gravel scattered at the bottom of a cage.

Perched on the spur, Bridgman felt a warning tremor of pain in his calf. He leapt down in a flurry of dust, without looking back made off among the dunes and reefs.

Later, as the last baroque whorls of the sunset faded below the horizon, he waited on the roof for Travis and Louise Woodward, peering impatiently into the empty moon-filled streets.

Shortly after midnight, at an elevation of 35 degrees in the south-west, between Aquila and Ophiuchus, the conjunction began. Bridgman continued to search the streets, and ignored the seven points of speeding light as they raced towards him from the horizon like an invasion from deep space. There was no indication of their convergent orbital pathways, which would soon scatter them thousands of miles apart, and the satellites moved as if they were always together, in the tight configuration Bridgman had known since childhood, like a lost zodiacal emblem, a constellation detached from the celestial sphere and forever frantically searching to return to its place.

"Travis! Confound you!" With a snarl, Bridgman swung away from the balcony and moved along to the exposed section of rail behind the elevator head. To be avoided like a pariah by Travis and Louise Woodward forced him to accept that he was no longer a true resident of the beach and now existed in a no-man's land between them and the wardens.

The seven satellites drew nearer, and Bridgman glanced up at them cursorily. They were disposed in a distinctive but unusual pattern resembling the Greek letter *khi,* a limp cross, a straight lateral member containing four capsules more or less in line ahead—Connolly, Tkachev, Merril and Maiakovski—bisected by three others forming with Tkachev an elongated Z—Pokrovski, Woodward and Brodisnek. The pattern had been variously identified as a hammer and sickle, an eagle, a swastika, and a dove, as well as a variety of religious and runic emblems, but all these were being defeated by the advancing tendency of the older capsules to vapourise.

It was this slow disintegration of the aluminum shells that made them visible—it had often been pointed out that the observer on the ground was looking, not at the actual capsule, but at a local field of vapourised aluminium and ionized hydrogen peroxide gas from the ruptured altitude jets now distributed within half a mile of each of the capsules. Woodward's, the most recently in orbit, was a barely perceptible point of light. The hulks of the capsules, with their perfectly preserved human cargoes, were continually dissolving, and a wide fan of silver spray opened out in a phantom wake behind Merril and Pokrovski (1998 and 1999), like a double star transforming itself into a nova in the centre of a constellation. As the mass of the capsules diminished they sank into a closer orbit around the earth, would soon touch the denser layers of the atmosphere and plummet to the ground.

Bridgman watched the satellites as they moved towards him, his irritation with Travis forgotten. As always, he felt himself moved by the eerie but strangely serene spectacle of the ghostly convoy endlessly circling the dark sea of the midnight sky, the long-dead astronauts converging for the ten-thousandth time upon their brief rendezvous and then setting off upon their lonely flight-paths around the perimeter of the ionosphere, the tidal edge of the beachway into space which had reclaimed them.

How Louise Woodward could bear to look up at her husband he had never been able to understand. After her arrival he once invited her to the hotel, remarking that there was an excellent view of the beautiful sunsets, and she had snapped back bitterly: "Beautiful? Can you imagine what it's like looking up at a sunset when your husband's spinning round through it in his coffin?"

This reaction had been a common one when the first astronauts had died after failing to make contact with the launching platforms in fixed orbit. When these new stars rose in the west an attempt had been made to shoot them down—there was the unsettling prospect of the skies a thousand years hence, littered with orbiting refuse—but later they were left in this natural graveyard, forming their own monument.

Obscured by the clouds of dust carried up into the air by the sand-storm, the satellites shone with little more than the intensity of second-magnitude stars, winking as the reflected light was interrupted by the lanes of strato-cirrus. The wake of diffusing light behind Merril and Pokrovski which usually screened the other capsules seemed to have diminished in size, and he could see both Maiakovski and Brodisnek clearly for the first time in several months. Wondering whether Merril or Pokrovski would be the first to fall from orbit, he looked towards the centre of the cross as it passed overhead.

With a sharp intake of breath, he tilted his head back. In surprise he noticed that one of the familiar points of light was missing from the centre of the group. What he had assumed to be an occlusion of the conjoint vapour trails by dust clouds was simply due to the fact that one of the capsules—Merril's, he decided, the third of the line ahead—had fallen from its orbit.

Head raised, he side-stepped slowly across the roof, avoiding the pieces of rusting neon sign, following the convoy as it passed overhead and moved towards the eastern horizon. No longer overlayed by the wake of Merril's capsule, Woodward's shone with far greater clarity, and almost appeared to have taken the former's place, although he was not due to fall from orbit for at least a century.

In the distance somewhere an engine growled. A moment later, from a different quarter, a woman's voice cried out faintly. Bridgman moved to the rail, over the intervening roof-tops saw two figures silhouetted against the sky on the elevator head of an apartment block, then heard Louise Woodward call out again. She was pointing up at the sky with both hands, her long hair blown about her face, Travis trying to restrain her. Bridgman realised that she had misconstrued Merril's descent, assuming that the fallen astronaut was her husband. He climbed on to the edge of the balcony, watching the pathetic tableau on the distant roof.

Again, somewhere among the dunes, an engine moaned. Before Bridgman could turn around, a brilliant blade of light cleaved the sky in the south-west. Like a speeding comet, an immense train of vapourising particles stretching behind it to the horizon, it soared towards them, the downward curve of its pathway clearly visible. Detached from the rest of the capsules, which were now disappearing among the stars along the eastern horizon, it was little more than a few miles off the ground.

Bridgman watched it approach, apparently on a collision course with the hotel. The expanding corona of white light, like a gigantic signal flare, illuminated the roof-tops, etching the letters of the neon signs over the submerged motels on the outskirts of the town. He ran for the doorway, as he raced down the stairs saw the glow of the descending capsule fill the sombre streets like a hundred moons. When he reached his room, sheltered by the massive weight of the hotel, he watched the dunes in front of the hotel light up like a stage set. Three hundred yards away the low camouflaged hull of the wardens' beach-car was revealed poised on a crest, its feeble spot-light drowned by the glare.

With a deep metallic sigh, the burning catafalque of the dead astronaut soared overhead, a cascade of vapourising metal pouring from its hull, filling the sky with incandescent light. Reflected below it, like an expressway illuminated by an aircraft's spot-lights, a long lane of light several hundred yards in width raced out into the desert towards the sea. As Bridgman shielded his eyes, it suddenly erupted in a tremendous explosion of detonating sand. A huge curtain of white dust lifted into the air and fell slowly to the ground. The sounds of the impact rolled against the hotel, mounting in a sustained crescendo that drummed against the windows. A series of smaller explosions flared up like opalescent fountains. All over the desert fires flickered briefly where fragments of the capsule had been scattered. Then the noise subsided, and an immense glistening pall of phosphorescing gas hung in the air like a silver veil, particles within it beading and winking.

Two hundred yards away across the sand was the running figure of Louise Woodward, Travis twenty paces behind her. Bridgman watched them dart in and out of the dunes, then abruptly felt the cold spot-light of the beach-car hit his face and flood the room behind him. The vehicle was moving straight towards him, two of the wardens, nets and lassoes in hand, riding the outboard.

Quickly Bridgman straddled the balcony, jumped down into the sand and raced towards the crest of the first dune. He crouched and ran on through the darkness as the beam probed the air. Above, the glistening pall was slowly fading, the particles of vapourised metal sifting towards the dark Martian sand. In the distance the last echoes of the impact were still reverberating among the hotels of the beach colonies further down the coast.

Five minutes later he caught up with Louise Woodward and Travis. The capsule's impact had flattened a number of the dunes, forming a shallow basin some quarter of a mile in diameter, and the surrounding slopes were scattered with the still glowing particles, sparkling like fading eyes. The beach-car growled somewhere four or five hundred yards behind him, and Bridgman broke off into an exhausted walk. He stopped beside Travis, who was kneeling on the ground, breath pumping into his lungs. Fifty yards away Louise Woodward was running up and down, distraughtly gazing at the fragments of smouldering metal. For a moment the spot-light of the approaching beach-car illuminated her, and she ran away among the dunes. Bridgman caught a glimpse of the inconsolable anguish in her face.

Travis was still on his knees. He had picked up a piece of the oxidised metal and was pressing it together in his hands.

"Travis, for God's sake tell her! This was Merril's capsule, there's no doubt about it! Woodward's still up there."

Travis looked up at him silently, his eyes searching Bridgman's face. A spasm of pain tore his mouth, and Bridgman realised that the barb of steel he clasped reverently in his hands was still glowing with heat.

"Travis!" He tried to pull the man's hands apart, the pungent stench of burning flesh gusting into his face, but Travis wrenched away from him. "Leave her alone, Bridgman! Go back with the wardens!"

Bridgman retreated from the approaching beach-car. Only thirty yards away, its spot-light filled the basin. Louise Woodward was still searching the dunes. Travis held his ground as the wardens jumped down from the car and advanced towards him with their nets, his bloodied hands raised at his sides, the steel barb flashing like a dagger. At the head of the wardens, the only one unmasked, was a trim, neat-featured man with an intent, serious face. Bridgman guessed that this was Major Webster, and that the wardens had known of the impending impact and hoped to capture them, and Louise in particular, before it occurred.

Bridgman stumbled back towards the dunes at the edge of the basin. As he neared the crest he trapped his foot in a semi-circular plate of metal, sat down and freed his heel.

Unmistakeably it was part of a control panel, the circular instrument housings still intact.

Overhead the pall of glistening vapour had moved off to the north-east, and the reflected light was directly over the rusting gantries of the former launching site at Cape Canaveral. For a few fleeting seconds the gantries seemed to be enveloped in a sheen of silver, transfigured by the vapourised body of the dead astronaut, diffusing over them in a farewell gesture, his final return to the site from which he had set off to his death a century earlier. Then the gantries sank again into their craggy shadows, and the pall moved off like an immense wraith towards the sea, barely distinguishable from the star glow.

Down below Travis was sitting on the ground surrounded by the wardens. He scuttled about on his hands like a frantic crab, scooping handfuls of the virus-laden sand at them. Holding tight to their masks, the wardens manoeuvred around him, their nets and lassoes at the ready. Another group moved slowly towards Bridgman.

Bridgman picked up a handful of the dark Martian sand beside the instrument panel, felt the soft glowing crystals warm his palm. In his mind he could still see the silver-sheathed gantries of the launching site across the bay, by a curious illusion almost identical with the Martian city he had designed years earlier. He watched the pall disappear over the sea, then looked around at the other remnants of Merril's capsule scattered over the slopes. High in the western night, between Pegasus and Cygnus, shone the distant disc of the planet Mars, which for both himself and the dead astronaut had served for so long as a symbol of unattained ambition. The wind stirred softly through the sand, cooling this replica of the planet which lay passively around him, and at last he understood why he had come to the beach and been unable to leave it.

Twenty yards away Travis was being dragged off like a wild dog, his thrashing body pinioned in the centre of a web of lassoes. Louise Woodward had run away among the dunes towards the sea, following the vanished gas cloud.

In a sudden excess of re-found confidence, Bridgman drove his fist into the dark sand, buried his forearm like a foundation pillar. A flange of hot metal from Merril's capsule burned his wrist bonding him to the spirit of the dead astronaut. Scattered around him on the Martian sand, in a sense Merril had reached Mars after all.

"Damn it!" he cried exultantly to himself as the wardens' lassoes stung his neck and shoulders. "We made it!"

PASSPORT TO ETERNITY

IT WAS half past love on New Day in Zenith and the clocks were striking heaven. All over the city the sounds of revelry echoed upwards into the dazzling Martian night, but high on Sunset Ridge, among the mansions of the rich, Margot and Clifford Gorrell faced each other in glum silence.

Frowning, Margot flipped impatiently through the vacation brochure on her lap, then tossed it away with an elaborate gesture of despair.

"But Clifford, why do we have to go to the same place every summer? I'd like to do something interesting for a change. This year the Lovatts are going to the Venus Fashion Festival, and Bobo and Peter Anders have just booked into the fire beaches at Saturn. They'll all have a wonderful time, while we're quietly taking the last boat to nowhere."

Clifford Gorrell nodded impassively, one hand cupped over the sound control in the arm of his chair. They had been arguing all evening, and Margot's voice threw vivid sparks of irritation across the walls and ceiling. Grey and mottled, they would take days to drain.

"I'm sorry you feel like that, Margot. Where would you like to go?"

Margot shrugged scornfully, staring out at the corona of a million neon signs that illuminated the city below. "Does it matter?"

"Of course. You arrange the vacation this time."

Margot hesitated, one eye keenly on her husband. Then she sat forward happily, turning up her fluorescent violet dress until she glowed like an Algolian rayfish.

"Clifford, I've got a wonderful idea! Yesterday I was down in the Colonial Bazaar, thinking about our holiday, when I found a small dream bureau that's just been opened. Something like the Dream Dromes in Neptune City everyone was crazy about two or three years ago, but instead of having to plug into whatever program happens to be going you have your own dream plays specially designed for you."

143

Clifford continued to nod, carefully increasing the volume of the sound-sweeper.

"They have their own studios and send along a team of analysts and writers to interview us and afterwards book a sanatorium anywhere we like for the convalescence. Eve Corbusier and I decided a small party of five or six would be best."

"Eve Corbusier," Clifford repeated. He smiled thinly to himself and switched on the book he had been reading. "I wondered when that gorgon was going to appear."

"Eve isn't too bad when you get to know her, darling," Margot told him. "Don't start reading yet. She'll think up all sorts of weird ideas for the play." Her voice trailed off. "What's the matter?"

"Nothing," Clifford said wearily. "It's just that I sometimes wonder if you have any sense of responsibility at all." As Margot's eyes darkened he went on. "Do you really think that I, a supreme court justice, could take that sort of vacation, even if I wanted to? Those dream plays are packed with advertising commercials and all sorts of corrupt material." He shook his head sadly. "And I told you not to go into the Colonial Bazaar."

"What are we going to do then?" Margot asked coldly. "Another honeyMoon?"

"I'll reserve a couple of singles tomorrow. Don't worry, you'll enjoy it." He clipped the hand microphone into his book and began to scan the pages with it, listening to the small metallic voice.

Margot stood up, the vanes in her hat quivering furiously. "Clifford!" she snapped, her voice dead and menacing. "I warn you, I'm not going on another honeyMoon!"

Absently, Clifford said: "Of course, dear," his fingers racing over the volume control.

"Clifford!"

Her shout sank to an angry squeak. She stepped over to him, her dress blazing like a dragon, jabbering at him noiselessly, the sounds sucked away through the vents over her head and pumped out across the echoing rooftops of the midnight city.

As he sat back quietly in his private vacuum, the ceiling shaking occasionally when Margot slammed a door upstairs, Clifford looked out over the brilliant diadem of down-town Zenith. In the distance, by the space-port, the ascending arcs of hyperliners flared across the sky while below the countless phosphorescent trajectories of hop-cabs enclosed the bowl of rooflight in a dome of glistening hoops.

Of all the cities of the galaxy, few offered such a wealth of pleasures as Zenith, but to Clifford Gorrell it was as distant and unknown as the first Gomorrah. At 35 he was a thin-faced, prematurely aging man with receding hair and a remote abstracted expression, and in the dark sombre suit and stiff white dog-collar which were the traditional uniform of the Probate Department's senior administrators he looked like a man who had never taken a holiday in his life.

At that moment Clifford wished he hadn't. He and Margot had never been able to agree about their vacations. Clifford's associates and superiors at the Department, all of them ten or twenty years older than himself, took their pleasures conservatively and expected a young but responsible justice to do the same. Margot grudgingly acknowledged this, but her friends who frequented the chic playtime clinics along the beach at Mira Mira considered the so-called honeyMoon trips back to Earth derisively old-fashioned, a last desperate resort of the aged and infirm.

And to tell the truth, Clifford realized, they were right. He had never dared to admit to Margot that he too was bored because it would have been more than his peace of mind was worth, but a change might do them good.

He resolved—next year.

Margot lay back among the cushions on the terrace divan, listening to the flamingo trees singing to each other in the morning sunlight. Twenty feet below, in the high-walled garden, a tall muscular young man was playing with a jet-ball. He had a dark olive complexion and swarthy good looks, and oil gleamed across his bare chest and arms. Margot watched with malicious amusement his efforts to entertain her. This was Trantino, Margot's play-boy, who chaperoned her during Clifford's long absences at the Probate Department.

"Hey, Margot! Catch!" He gestured with the jet-ball but Margot turned away, feeling her swim-suit slide pleasantly across her smooth tanned skin. The suit was made of one of the newer bioplastic materials, and its living tissues were still growing, softly adapting themselves to the contours of her body, repairing themselves as the fibres became worn or grimy. Upstairs in her wardrobes the gowns and dresses purred on their hangars like the drowsing inmates of some exquisite arboreal zoo. Sometimes she thought of commissioning her little Mercurian tailor to run up a bioplastic suit for Clifford—a specially designed suit that would begin to constrict one night as he stood on the terrace, the lapels growing tighter and tighter around his neck, the sleeves pinning his arms to his sides, the waist contracting to pitch him over—

"Margot!" Trantino interrupted her reverie, sailed the jet-ball expertly through the air towards her. Annoyed, Margot caught it with one hand and pointed it away, watched it sail over the wall and the roofs beyond.

Trantino came up to her. "What's the matter?" he asked anxiously. For his part he felt his inability to soothe Margot a reflection on his professional skill. The privileges of his caste had to be guarded jealously. For several centuries now the managerial and technocratic elite had been so preoccupied with the work of government that they relied on the Templars of Aphrodite not merely to guard their wives from any marauding suitors but also to keep them amused and contented. By definition, of course, their relationship was platonic, a pleasant revival of the old chivalrous ideals, but sometimes Trantino regretted that the only tools in his armory were a handful of poems and empty romantic gestures. The Guild of which he was a novitiate member was an ancient and honored one, and it wouldn't do if Margot began to pine and Mr. Gorrell reported him to the Masters of the Guild.

"Why are you always arguing with Mr. Gorrell?" Trantino asked her. One of the Guild's axioms was 'The husband is *always* right.' Any discord between him and his wife was the responsibility of the play-boy.

Margot ignored Trantino's question. "Those trees are getting on my nerves," she complained fractiously. "Why can't they keep quiet?"

"They're mating," Trantino told her. He added thoughtfully: "You should sing to Mr. Gorrell."

Margot stirred lazily as the shoulder straps of the sun-suit unclasped themselves behind her back. "Tino," she asked, "What's the most unpleasant thing I could do to Mr. Gorrell?"

"Margot!" Trantino gasped, utterly shocked. He decided that an appeal to sentiment, a method of reconciliation despised by the more proficient members of the Guild, was his only hope. "Remember, Margot, you will always have me."

He was about to permit himself a melancholy smile when Margot sat up abruptly.

"Don't look so frightened, you fool! I've just got an idea that should make Mr. Gorrell sing to me."

She straightened the vanes in her hat, waited for the sun-suit to clasp itself discreetly around her, then pushed Trantino aside and stalked off the terrace.

Clifford was browsing among the spools in the library, quietly listening to an old 22nd Century abstract on systems of land tenure in the Trianguli.

"Hello, Margot, feel better now?"

Margot smiled at him coyly. "Clifford, I'm ashamed of myself. Do forgive me." She bent down and nuzzled his ear. "Sometimes I'm very selfish. Have you booked our tickets yet?"

Clifford disengaged her arm and straightened his collar. "I called the agency, but their bookings have been pretty heavy. They've got a double but no singles. We'll have to wait a few days."

"No, we won't," Margot exclaimed brightly. "Clifford, why don't you and I take the double? Then we can really be together, forget all that ship-board nonsense about never having met before."

Puzzled, Clifford switched off the player. "What do you mean?"

Margot explained. "Look, Clifford, I've been thinking that I ought to spend more time with you than I do at present, really share your work and hobbies. I'm tired of all these play-boys." She drooped languidly against Clifford, her voice silky and reassuring. "I want to be with you, Clifford. *Always*."

Clifford pushed her away. "Don't be silly, Margot," he said with an anxious laugh. "You're being absurd."

"No, I'm not. After all, Harold Kharkov and his wife haven't got a play-boy and she's very happy."

Maybe she is, Clifford thought, beginning to panic. Kharkov had once been the powerful and ruthless director of the Department of Justice, now was a third-rate attorney hopelessly trying to eke out a meagre living on the open market, dominated by his wife and forced to spend virtually 24 hours a day with her. For a moment Clifford thought of the days when he had courted Margot, of the long dreadful hours listening to her inane chatter. Trantino's real role was not to chaperone Margot while Clifford was away but while he was at home.

"Margot, be sensible," he started to say, but she cut him short. "I've made up my mind, I'm going to tell Trantino to pack his suitcase and go back to the Guild." She switched on the spool player, selecting the wrong speed, smiling ecstatically as the reading head grated loudly and stripped the coding off the record. "It's going to be wonderful to share everything with you. Why don't we forget about the vacation this year?"

A facial tic from which Clifford had last suffered at the age of ten began to twitch ominously.

Tony Harcourt, Clifford's personal assistant, came over to the Gorrell's villa immediately after lunch. He was a brisk, polished young man, barely controlling his annoyance at being called back to work on the first day of his vacation. He had carefully booked a sleeper next to Dolores Costane, the most beautiful of the Jovian Heresiarch's vestals, on board a leisure-liner leaving that afternoon for Venus, but instead of enjoying the fruits of weeks of blackmail and intrigue he was having to take part in what seemed a quite uncharacteristic piece of Gorrell whimsy.

He listened in growing bewilderment as Clifford explained.

"We were going to one of our usual resorts on Luna, Tony, but we've decided we need a change. Margot wants a vacation that's different. Something new, exciting, original. So go round all the agencies and bring me their suggestions."

"All the agencies?" Tony queried. "Don't you mean just the registered ones?"

"All of them," Margot told him smugly, relishing every moment of her triumph.

Clifford nodded, and smiled at Margot benignly.

"But there must be 50 or 60 agencies organizing vacations," Tony protested. "Only about a dozen of them are accredited. Outside Empyrean Tours and Union-Galactic there'll be absolutely nothing suitable for you."

"Never mind," Clifford said blandly. "We only want an idea of the field. I'm sorry, Tony, but I don't want this all over the Department and I know you'll be discreet."

Tony groaned. "It'll take me weeks."

"Three days," Clifford told him. "Margot and I want to leave here by the end of the week." He looked longingly over his shoulder for the absent Trantino. "Believe me, Tony, we really need a holiday."

Fifty-six travel and vacation agencies were listed in the Commercial Directory, Tony discovered when he returned to his office in the top floor of the Justice building in downtown Zenith, all but eight of them alien. The Department had initiated legal proceedings against five, three had closed down, and eight more were fronts for other enterprises.

That left him with forty to visit, spread all over the Upper and Lower Cities and in the Colonial Bazaar, attached to various mercantile, religious and paramilitary organizations, some of them huge concerns with their own police and ecclesiastical forces, others sharing a one-room office and transceiver with a couple of other shoestring firms.

Tony mapped out an itinerary, slipped a flask of Five-Anchor Neptunian Rum into his hip pocket and dialled a helicab.

The first was ARCO PRODUCTIONS INC., a large establishment occupying three levels and a bunker on the fashionable west side of the Upper City. According to the Directory they specialized in hunting and shooting expeditions.

The helicab put him down on the apron outside the entrance. Massive steel columns reached up to a reinforced concrete portico, and the whole place looked less like a travel agency than the last redoubt of some interstellar Seigfreid. As he went in a smart jackbooted guard of janissaries in black and silver uniforms snapped to attention and presented arms.

Everyone inside the building was wearing a uniform, moving about busily at standby alert. A huge broad-shouldered woman with sergeant's stripes handed Tony over to a hard-faced Martian colonel.

"I'm making some inquiries on behalf of a wealthy Terran and his wife," Tony explained. "They thought they'd do a little big-game hunting on their vacation this year. I believe you organize expeditions."

The colonel nodded curtly and led Tony over to a broad map-table. "Certainly. What exactly have they in mind?"

"Well, nothing really. They hoped you'd make some suggestions."

"Of course." The colonel pulled out a memo-tape. "Have they their own air and land forces?"

Tony shook his head. "I'm afraid not."

"I see. Can you tell me whether they will require a single army corps, a combined task force or—"

"No," Tony said. "Nothing as big as that."

"An assault party of brigade strength? I understand. Quieter and less elaborate. All the fashion today." He switched on the star-map and spread his hands across the glimmering screen of stars and nebulae. "Now the question of the particular theatre. At present only three of the game reserves have open seasons. Firstly the Procyon system; this includes about 20 different races, some of them still with only atomic technologies. Unfortunately there's been a good deal of dispute recently about declaring Procyon a game reserve, and the Resident of Alschain is trying to have it admitted to the Pan-Galactic Conference. A pity, I feel," the colonel added, reflectively stroking his steel-grey moustache.

"Procyon always put up a great fight against us and an expedition there was invariably lively."

Tony nodded sympathetically. "I hadn't realized they objected."

The colonel glanced at him sharply. "Naturally," he said. He cleared his throat. "That leaves only the Ketab tribes of Ursa Major, who are having their Millennial Wars, and the Sudor Martines of Orion. They are an entirely new reserve, and your best choice without doubt. The ruling dynasty died out recently, and a war of succession could be conveniently arranged."

Tony was no longer following the colonel, but he smiled intelligently.

"Now," the colonel asked, "what political or spiritual creeds do your friends wish to have invoked?"

Tony frowned. "I don't think they want any. Are they absolutely necessary?"

The colonel regarded Tony carefully. "No," he said slowly. "It's a question of taste. A purely military operation is perfectly feasible. However, we always advise our clients to invoke some doctrine as a *casus belli*, not only to avoid adverse publicity and any feelings of guilt or remorse, but to lend color and purpose to the campaign. Each of our field commanders specializes in a particular ideological pogrom, with the exception of General Westerling. Perhaps your friends would prefer him?"

Tony's mind started to work again. "Schapiro Westerling? The former Director-General of Graves Commission?"

The colonel nodded. "You know him?"

Tony laughed. "Know him? I thought I was prosecuting him at the current Nova Trials. I can see that we're well behind with the times." He pushed back his chair. "To tell the truth I don't think you've anything suitable for my friends. Thanks all the same."

The colonel stiffened. One of his hands moved below the desk and a buzzer sounded along the wall.

"However," Tony added, "I'd be grateful if you'd send them further details."

The colonel sat impassively in his chair. Three enormous guards appeared at Tony's elbow, idly swinging energy truncheons.

"Clifford Gorrell, Stellar Probate Division, Department of Justice," Tony said quickly.

He gave the colonel a brief smile and made his way out, cursing Clifford and walking warily across the thickly-piled carpet in case it had been mined.

The next one on his list was the A-Z JOLLY JUBILEE COMPANY, alien and unregistered, head office somewhere out of Betelgeuse. According to the Directory they specialized in 'all-in cultural parties and guaranteed somatic weekends.' Their premises occupied the top two tiers of a hanging garden in the Colonial Bazaar. They sounded harmless enough but Tony was ready for them.

"No," he said firmly to a lovely Antarean wraith-fern who shyly raised a frond to him as he crossed the terrace. "Not today."

Behind the bar a fat man in an asbestos suit was feeding sand to a siliconic fire-fish swimming round in a pressure brazier.

"Damn things," he grumbled, wiping the sweat off his chin and fiddling aimlessly with the thermostat. "They gave me a booklet when I got it, but it doesn't say anything about it eating a whole beach every day." He spaded in another couple of shovels from a low dune of sand heaped on the floor behind him. "You have to keep them at exactly $5750°K.$ or they start getting nervous. Can I help you?"

"I thought there was a vacation agency here," Tony said.

"Sure. I'll call the girls for you." He pressed a bell.

"Wait a minute," Tony cut in. "You advertise something about cultural parties. What exactly are they?"

The fat man chuckled. "That must be my partner. He's a professor at Vega Tech. Likes to keep the tone up." He winked at Tony.

Tony sat on one of the stools, looking out over the crazy spiral roof-tops of the Bazaar. A mile away the police patrols circled over the big apartment batteries which marked the perimeter of the Bazaar, keeping their distance.

A tall slim woman appeared from behind the foliage and sauntered across the terrace to him. She was a Canopan slave, hot-housed out of imported germ, a slender green-skinned beauty with moth-like fluttering gills.

The fat man introduced Tony. "Lucille, take him up to the arbour and give him a run through."

Tony tried to protest but the pressure brazier was hissing fiercely. The fat man started feeding sand in furiously, the exhaust flames flaring across the terrace.

Quickly, Tony turned and backed up the stairway to the arbour. "Lucille," he reminded her firmly, "this is strictly cultural, remember."

Half an hour later a dull boom reverberated up from the terrace.

"Poor Jumbo," Lucille said sadly as a fine rain of sand came down over them.

"Poor Jumbo," Tony agreed, sitting back and playing with a coil of her hair. Like a soft sinuous snake, it circled around his arm, sleek with blue oil. He drained the flask of Five-Anchor and tossed it lightly over the balustrade. "Now tell me more about these Canopan prayerbeds. . . ."

When, after two days, Tony reported back to the Gorrells he looked hollow-eyed and exhausted, like a man who had been brain-washed by the Wardens.

"What happened to you?" Margot asked anxiously, "we thought you'd been going round the agencies."

"Exactly," Tony said. He slumped down in a sofa and tossed a thick folder across to Clifford. "Take your pick. You've got about 250 schemes there in complete detail, but I've written out a synopsis which gives one or two principal suggestions from each agency. Most of them are out of the question."

Clifford unclipped the synopsis and started to read through it.

(1) ARCO PRODUCTIONS INC. Unregistered. Private subsidiary of Sagittarius Security Police.

Hunting and shooting. Your own war to order. Raiding parties, revolutions, religious crusades. In anything from a small commando squad to a 3,000-ship armada. ARCO provide publicity, mock War Crimes Tribunal, etc. Samples:

(a) Operation Torquemada. 23-day expedition to Bellatrix IV. 20-ship assault corps under Admiral Storm Wengen. Mission: liberation of (imaginary) Terran hostages. Cost: 300,000 credits.

(b) Operation Klingsor. 15-year crusade against Ursa Major. Combined task force of 2,500 ships. Mission: recovery of runic memory dials stolen from client's shrine.

Cost: 500 billion credits (ARCO will arrange lend-lease but this is dabbling in realpolitik).

(2) ARENA FEATURES INC. Unregistered. Organizers of the Pan-Galactic Tournament held tri-millennially at the Sun Bowl, 2-Heliopolis, NGC 3599.

Every conceivable game in the Cosmos is played at the tournament and so formidable is the opposition that a winning contestant can virtually choose his own apotheosis. The challenge round of the Solar Megathlon, Group 3 (that is, for any being whose function can be described, however loosely, as living) involves Quantum Jumping, 7-dimensional Maze Ball and Psychokinetic Bridge (pretty tricky against a telepathic Ketos D'Oma). The only Terran ever to win an event was the redoubtable Chippy Yerkes of Altair 5 The Clowns, who introduced the unplayable blank Round Dice. Being a spectator is as exhausting as being a contestant, and you're well advised to substitute.

Cost: 100,000 credits/day.

(3) AGENCE GENERALE DE TOURISME. Registered. Venus.

Concessionaires for the Colony Beatific on Lake Virgo, the Mandrake Casino Circuit and the Miramar-Trauma Senso-channels. Dream-baths, vu-dromes, endocrine-galas. Darleen Costello is the current Aphrodite and Laurence Mandell makes a versatile Lothario. Plug into these two from 30:30 VST. Room and non-denominational bath at the Gomorrah-Plaza on Mount Venus comes to 1,000 credits a day, but remember to keep out of the Zone. It's just too erotogenous for a Terran.

(4) TERMINAL TOURS LTD. Unregistered. Earth.

For those who want to get away from it all the *Dream of Osiris,* an astral-rigged, 1,000-foot leisure-liner is now fitting out for the Grand Tour. Round-cosmos cruise, visiting every known race and galaxy.

Cost: Doubles at a flat billion, but it's cheap when you realize that the cruise lasts for ever and you'll never be back.

(5) SLEEP TRADERS, Unregistered.

A somewhat shadowy group who handle all dealings on the Blue Market, acting as a general clearing house and buying and selling dreams all through the Galaxy.

Sample: Like to try a really new sort of dream? The Set Corrani Priests of Theta Piscium will link you up with the sacred electronic thought-pools in the Desert of Kish. These mercury lakes are their ancestral memory banks. Surgery is necessary but be careful. Too much cortical damage and the archetypes may get restive. In return one of the Set Corrani (polysexual delta-humanoids about the size of a walking dragline) will take over your cerebral functions for a long weekend. All these transactions are done on an exchange basis and SLEEP TRADERS charge nothing for the service. But they obviously get a rake-off, and may pump advertising into the lower medullary centres. Whatever they're selling I wouldn't advise anybody to buy.

(6) THE AGENCY. Registered. M33 in Andromeda.

The executive authority of the consortium of banking trusts floating Schedule D, the fourth draw of the gigantic PK pyramid lottery sweeping all through the continuum from Sol III out to the island universes. Trance-cells everywhere are now recruiting dream-readers and ESPerceptionists, and there's still time to buy a ticket. There's only one number on all the tickets—the winning one—but don't think that means you'll get away with the kitty. THE AGENCY has just launched UNILIV, the emergency relief fund for victims of Schedule C who lost their deposits and are now committed to paying off impossible debts, some monetary, some moral (if you're unlucky in the draw you may find yourself landed with a guilt complex that would make even a Colonus Rex look sad.)

Cost: 1 credit—but with an evaluation in the billions if you have to forfeit.

(7) ARCTURIAN EXPRESS. Unregistered.

Controls all important track events. The racing calendar this year is a causal and not a temporal one and seems a little obscure, but most of the established classics are taking place.

(a) The Rhinosaur Derby. Held this year at Betelgeuse Springs under the rules of the Federation of Amorphs. First to the light horizon. There's always quite a line-up for this one and any form of vehicle is allowed—rockets, beams, racial migrations, ES thought patterns—but frankly it's a waste of effort. It's not just that by the time you're out of your own sight you're usually out of your mind as well, but the Nils of Rigel, who always enter a strong team, are capable of instantaneous transmission.

(b) The Paraplegic Handicap. Recently instituted by the Protists of Lambda Scorpio. The course measures only 0.00015 mm., but that's a long way to urge an Aldebaran Torpid. They are giant viruses embedded in bauxite mountains, and by varying their pressure differentials it's sometimes possible to tickle them into a little life. K 2 on Regulus IX is holding the big bets, but even so the race is estimated to take about 50,000 years to run.

(8) NEW FUTURES INC. Unregistered.

Tired of the same dull round? NEW FUTURES will take you right out of this world. In the island universes the continuum is extra-dimensional, and the time channels are controlled by rival cartels. The element of chance apparently plays the time role, and it's all even more confused by the fact that you may be moving around in someone else's extrapolation.

In the tourist translation manual 185 basic tenses are given, and of these 125 are future conditional. No verb conjugates in the present tense, and you can invent and copyright your own irregulars. This may explain why I got the impression at the bureau that they were only half there.

Cost: simultaneously 3, 270 and 2,000,000 credits. They refuse to quibble.

(9) SEVEN SIRENS. Registered. Venus.

A subsidiary of the fashion trust controlling senso-channel Astral Eve.

Ladies, like to win your own beauty contest? Twenty-five of the most beautiful creatures in the Galaxy are waiting to pit their charms against yours, but however divine they may be—and two or three of them, such as the Flamen Zilla Quel-Queen (75-9-25) and the Orthodox Virgin of Altair (76-953-?) certainly will be—they'll stand no chance against you. Your specifications will be defined as the ideal ones.

(10) GENERAL ENTERPRISES INC. Registered.

Specialists in culture cycles, world struggles, ethnic trends. Organize vacations as a sideline. A vast undertaking for whom ultimately we all work. Their next venture, epoch-making by all accounts, is starting now, and everybody will be coming along. I was politely but firmly informed that it was no use worrying about the cost. When I asked—

Before Clifford could finish one of the houseboys came up to him.

"Priority Call for you, sir."

Clifford handed the synopsis to Margot. "Tell me if you find anything. It looks to me as if we've been wasting Tony's time."

He left them and went through to his study.

"Ah, Gorrell, here you are." It was Thornwall Harrison, the attorney who had taken over Clifford's office. "Who the hell are all these people trailing in to see you night and day? The place looks like Colonial Night at the Arena Circus. I can't get rid of them."

"Which people?" Clifford asked. "What do they want?"

"You, apparently," Thornwall told him. "Most of them thought I was you. They've been trying to sell me all sorts of crazy vacation schemes. I said you'd already gone on your vacation and I myself never took one. Then one of them pulled a hypodermic on me. There's even an Anti-Cartel agent sleuthing around, wants to see you about block bookings. Thinks you're a racketeer."

Back in the lounge Margot and Tony were looking out

through the terrace windows into the boulevard which ran
from the Gorrell's villa to the level below.

A long column of vehicles had pulled up under the trees:
trucks, half-tracks, huge Telesenso studio location vans and
several sleek white ambulances. The drivers and crew-men
were standing about in little groups in the shadows, quietly
watching the villa. Two or three radar scanners on the vans
were rotating, and as Clifford looked down a convoy of trucks
drove up and joined the tail of the column.

"Looks like there's going to be quite a party," Tony said.
"What are they waiting for?"

"Perhaps they've come for us?" Margot suggested excitedly.

"They're wasting their time if they have," Clifford told her.
He swung round on Tony. "Did you give our names to any
of the agencies?"

Tony hesitated, then nodded. "I couldn't help it. Some of
those outfits wouldn't take no for an answer."

Clifford clamped his lips and picked the synopsis off the
floor. "Well, Margot, have you decided where you want to
go?"

Margot fiddled with the synopsis. "There are so many to
choose from."

Tony started for the door. "Well, I'll leave you to it." He
waved a hand at them. "Have fun."

"Hold on," Clifford told him. "Margot hasn't made up her
mind yet."

"What's the hurry?" Tony asked. He indicated the line of
vehicles outside, their crews now climbing into their driving
cabs and turrets. "Take your time. You may bite off more
than you can chew."

"Exactly. So as soon as Margot decides where we're going
you can make the final arrangements for us and get rid of
that menagerie."

"But Clifford, give me a chance."

"Sorry. Now Margot, hurry up."

Margot flipped through the synopsis, screwing up her
mouth. "It's so difficult, Clifford, I don't really like any of
these. I still think the best agency was the little one I found
in the Bazaar."

"No," Tony groaned, sinking down on a sofa. "Margot,
please, after all the trouble I've gone to."

"Yes, definitely that one. The dream bureau. What was it
called—"

Before she could finish there was a roar of engines starting up in the boulevard. Startled, Clifford saw the column of
cars and trucks churn across the gravel towards the villa.

Music, throbbing heavily, came down from the room above, and a sick musky odor seeped through the air.

Tony pulled himself off the sofa. "They must have had this place wired," he said quickly. "You'd better call the police. Believe me, some of these people don't waste time arguing."

Outside three helmeted men in brown uniforms ran past the terrace, unwinding a coil of fuse wire. The sharp hissing sound of para-rays sucked through the air from the drive.

Margot hid back in her slumber seat. "Trantino!" she wailed.

Clifford went back into his study. He switched the transceiver to the emergency channel.

Instead of the police signal a thin automatic voice beeped through. "Remain seated, remain seated. Take-off in zero two minutes, Purser's office on G Deck now——"

Clifford switched to another channel. There was a blare of studio applause and a loud unctuous voice called out:

"And now over to brilliant young Clifford Gorrell and his charming wife Margot about to enter their dream-pool at the fabulous Riviera-Neptune. Are you there, Cliff?"

Angrily, Clifford turned to a third. Static and morse chattered, and then someone rapped out in a hard iron tone: "Colonel Sapt is dug in behind the swimming pool. Enfilade along the garage roof——"

Clifford gave up. He went back to the lounge. The music was deafening. Margot was prostrate in her slumber-seat, Tony down on the floor by the window, watching a pitched battle raging in the drive. Heavy black palls of smoke drifted across the terrace, and two tanks with stylized archers emblazoned on their turrets were moving up past the burning wrecks of the studio location vans.

"They must be Arco's!" Tony shouted. "The police will look after them, but wait until the extra-sensory gang take over!"

Crouching behind a low stone parapet running off the terrace was a group of waiters in dishevelled evening dress, lab technicians in scorched white overalls and musicians clutching their instrument cases. A bolt of flame from one of the tanks flickered over their heads and crashed into the grove of flamingo trees, sending up a shower of sparks and broken notes.

Clifford pulled Tony to his feet. "Come on, we've got to get out of here. We'll try the library windows into the garden. You'd better take Margot."

Her yellow beach robe had apparently died of shock, and was beginning to blacken like a dried-out banana skin. Discreetly averting his eyes, Tony picked her up and followed Clifford out into the hall.

Three croupiers in gold uniforms were arguing hotly with two men in white surgeons' coats. Behind them a couple of mechanics were struggling a huge vibrobath up the stairs.

The foreman came over to Clifford. "Gorrell?" he asked, consulting an invoice. "Trans-Ocean." He jerked a thumb at the bath. "Where do you want it?"

A surgeon elbowed him aside. "Mr. Gorrell?" he asked suavely. "We are from Cerebro-Tonic Travel. Please allow me to give you a sedative. All this noise—"

Clifford pushed past him and started to walk down the corridor to the library, but the floor began to slide and weave.

He stopped and looked around unsteadily.

Tony was down on his knees, Margot flopped out of his arms across the floor.

Someone swayed up to Clifford and held out a tray.

On it were three tickets.

Around him the walls whirled.

He woke in his bedroom, lying comfortably on his back, gently breathing a cool amber air. The noise had died away, but he could still hear a vortex of sound spinning violently in the back of his mind. It spiralled away, vanished, and he moved his head and looked around.

Margot was lying asleep beside him, and for a moment he thought that the attack on the house had been a dream. Then he noticed the skull-plate clamped over his head, and the cables leading off from a boom to a large console at the foot of the bed. Massive spools loaded with magnetic tape waited in the projector ready to be played.

The real nightmare was still to come! He struggled to get up, found himself clamped in a twilight sleep, unable to move more than a few centimetres.

He lay there powerlessly for ten minutes, tongue clogging his mouth like a wad of cotton-wool when he tried to shout. Eventually a small neatly featured alien in a pink silk suit opened the door and padded quietly over to them. He peered down at their faces and then turned a couple of knobs on the console.

Clifford's consciousness began to clear. Beside him Margot stirred and woke.

The alien beamed down pleasantly. "Good evening," he greeted them in a smooth creamy voice. "Please allow me to apologize for any discomfort you have suffered. However, the first day of a vacation is often a little confused."

Margot sat up. "I remember you. You're from the little

bureau in the Bazaar." She jumped round happily. "Clifford!"

The alien bowed. "Of course, Mrs. Gorrell. I am Dr. Terence Sotal-2 Burlington, Professor—Emeritus," he added to himself as an afterthought, "—of Applied Drama at the University of Alpha Leporis, and the director of the play you and your husband are to perform during your vacation."

Clifford cut in: "Would you release me from this machine immediately? And then get out of my house! I've had—"

"Clifford!" Margot snapped. "What's the matter with you?"

Clifford dragged at the skull plate and Dr. Burlington quietly moved a control on the console. Part of Clifford's brain clouded and he sank back helplessly.

"Everything is all right, Mr. Gorrell," Dr. Burlington said.

"Clifford," Margot warned him. "Remember your promise." She smiled at Dr. Burlington. "Don't pay any attention to him, Doctor. Please go on."

"Thank you, Mrs. Gorrell." Dr. Burlington bowed again, as Clifford lay half-asleep, groaning impotently.

"The play we have designed for you," Dr. Burlington explained, "is an adaptation of a classic masterpiece in the Diphenyl 2-4-6 Cyclopropane canon, and though based on the oldest of human situations, is nonetheless fascinating. It was recently declared the outright winner at the Mira Nuptial Contest, and will always have a proud place in the private repertoires. To you, I believe, it is known as 'The Taming of the Shrew.'"

Margot giggled and then looked surprised. Dr. Burlington smiled urbanely. "However, allow me to show you the script." He excused himself and slipped out.

Margot fretted anxiously, while Clifford pulled weakly at the skull-plate.

"Clifford, I'm not sure that I like this altogether. And Dr. Burlington does seem rather strange. But I suppose it's only for three weeks."

Just then the door opened and a stout bearded figure, erect in a stiff blue uniform, white yachting cap jauntily on his head, stepped in.

"Good evening, Mrs. Gorrell." He saluted Margot smartly, "Captain Linstrom." He looked down at Clifford. "Good to have you aboard, sir."

"Aboard?" Clifford repeated weakly. He looked around at the familiar furniture in the room, the curtains drawn neatly over the windows. "What are you raving about? Get out of my house!"

The Captain chuckled. "Your husband has a sense of humor, Mrs. Gorrell. A useful asset on these long trips.

Your friend Mr. Harcourt in the next cabin seems sadly lacking in one."

"Tony?" Margot exclaimed. "Is he still here?"

Captain Linstrom laughed. "I quite understand you. He seems very worried, quite over-eager to return to Mars. We shall be passing there one day, of course, though not I fear for some time. However, time is no longer a consideration to you. I believe you are to spend the entire voyage in sleep. But a very pleasantly colored sleep nonetheless." He smiled roguishly at Margot.

As he reached the door Clifford managed to gasp out: "Where are we? For heaven's sake, call the police!"

Captain Linstrom paused in surprise. "But surely you know, Mr. Gorrell?" He strode to the window and flung back the curtains. In place of the large square casement were three small portholes. Outside a blaze of incandescent light flashed by, a rush of stars and nebulae.

Captain Linstrom gestured theatrically. "This is the *Dream of Osiris,* under charter to Terminal Tours, three hours out from Zenith City on the non-stop run. May I wish you sweet dreams!"